The Nightcharmer and Other Tales of Claude Seignolle

The Nightcharmer
and Other Tales of
Claude Seignolle

Edited and translated with an introduction by
Eric Hollingsworth Deudon

Foreword by Lawrence Durrell
Drawings by Kristin Parsons

TEXAS A&M UNIVERSITY PRESS
College Station

Library of Congress Cataloging in Publication Data

Seignolle, Claude.
The nightcharmer and other tales of Claude Seignolle.

Bibliography: p.
Contents: The nightcharmer—A dog story—The
healer—[etc.]
1. Seignolle, Claude—Translations, English.
2. Horror tales, French—Translations into English.
3. Horror tales, English—Translations from French.
I. Deudon, Eric Hollingsworth. II. Title.
PQ2637.E39A23   1983   843'.912   83-45104
ISBN 0-89096-169-7

Manufactured in the United States of America
FIRST EDITION

Contents

Foreword 7

Introduction 9

The Nightcharmer 15

A Dog Story 25

The Healer 31

Starfish 39

The Outlander 45

The Last Rites 85

Hitching a Ride 94

Night Horses 101

Selected Bibliography 113

Foreword

THE invitation to write a foreword to the first English translation of Claude Seignolle's tales could not be more opportune. I have long struggled against the apathy and the lack of imagination of British publishers—vainly hoping to interest them in these unique, macabre, and demoniac stories.

Claude Seignolle's work could be characterized by suggesting that it belongs to the Anglo-Germanic Gothic tradition—to the lineage of Ernst Hoffman, Anne Radcliffe, and Mary Shelley. But it is more than that. The particular nature of Seignolle's stories separates him from these authors. He brings into play authentic material and real-life subjects, not just fictitious characters. Glancing through one of Seignolle's huge compilations on French folklore, any reader would understand that the werewolf and the vampire are as alive today in the rustic mind as they were in the past. He would also realize that even though Seignolle's books can be read as works of fiction, they actually reveal to some of us a most disquieting and personal message. And perhaps it is that new awareness that might lead the reader to wonder if. . .

The sorcerers are still alive today, acting invisibly on the secret life of man: they are not the dead subject matter of scholarship alone, but also fitting material for the poet who is always turning over the stones of the human mind to see what might lie underneath. It does not take long to become completely seduced, completely *Seignollisé*. It is this curious taste of mystery that gives him poetic density in his work, even when he is writing of things very far removed from the diabolical. For example, in *La Gueule*, his war memoirs, there is little enough about vampires or such matters; but the tone of his prose charges the atmosphere with the feeling of poetry and mystery. Poetic mystery hangs like a mist over his work. And yet—diable!—he is not dreamy, diffuse, sentimental; he is gay, strong, truthful, and intense.

In the actual execution of Seignolle there is a very special quality that comes, I believe, from the fact that he is a Frenchman and neither a German nor an Englishman; he treats his frightening subject matter with a rather terrifying lucidity and intellectual control that makes it most convincing. He is of course a born storyteller, but you never feel with his work (as you so often do with the Gothic school) that the writer has set out to *épater* you, or to frighten you.

The short stories here assembled and translated by Professor Deudon will widen the circle of those of us who like Gothic tales. I can predict that Claude Seignolle will draw a large audience in the United States and that his place in literature eventually will be as assured as Ambrose Bierce's is today.

Lawrence Durrell

Introduction

IN 1976, les Presses de la Renaissance in Paris undertook the publication of Claude Seignolle's complete fiction works—a task of some magnitude, since this new edition comprised twenty-three volumes. But though Seignolle's works have already been translated into eight languages, adapted for both theater and cinema, and chosen as the topic of more than one hundred literary articles, books, essays, and theses, they still remain practically unknown in the United States.

Several reasons can be found for this oversight: first, his writings have long awaited an English translation to make them available to the American public. Another reason, more subtle perhaps, concerns the author's orientation—that of an untiring and thorough exploration of the fantastic. The very nature of this subject matter seems to have predisposed certain critics to confine Seignolle's books within the lesser category of popular literature, thereby strengthening a prevailing contemporary attitude that offhandedly banishes the bizarre and the unearthly from the spheres of "literary respectability." Lawrence Durrell readily discerned the critics' biases when he wrote, "It is the diversity of his gifts and talent which have so far deprived Seignolle of the popularity his works deserve. His own particular blend of poetry, mystery and irony places him outside and above contemporary writers."[1]

If Seignolle's fiction is still being ignored by many modern literature scholars, his name is not unfamiliar to Ameri-

[1] Foreword to Seignolle's *Un Corbeau de toutes couleurs*.

can ethnologists. As a life member of the prestigious Société
Préhistorique Française, into which he was inducted by Teil-
hard de Chardin, Seignolle published his first scholarly book
in 1937, at the age of twenty.[2] Collaborating with Professor
Van Gennep, he wrote several definitive reference books on
French folklore (*Les Fouilles de Robinson*, 1945; *En Sologne*,
1945; *Le Folklore du Languedoc*, 1960; *Le Folklore de la Provence*,
1963; *Le Berry traditionnel*, 1969; *Histoires et légendes de la Gascogne et de la Guyenne mystérieuses*, 1973).

Seignolle's first incursion into literature dates back to
1945 when he published his first novel,[3] followed in 1958 by
his first short story.[4] From that time on he wrote more than
twenty consecutive volumes.

Two distinct types of short stories can be identified in
Seignolle's writings: the "rustic" tale, which depicts folklore
traditions by inducting the reader into the particular and
eerie confines of the French countryside; and the "modern"
narrative, in which primitive topics such as superstitions and
black magic come alive within our contemporary society.
Thus the reader will not be surprised to encounter such pro-
tagonists as the werewolf, the damned, and a whole retinue
of the creatures of the night. The author, however, does not
portray them merely as frightening characters, for the total-
ity of these themes represents a direct transposition from his
research on folklore into the literary domain. The sorcerer
and the accursed belong to ancient traditions, to which Seignolle has devoted a substantial part of his ethnological research. All are revived for a moment and depicted with the
same fervor that still keeps them alive today among many
residents of the French countryside. Seignolle does not write
Gothic tales simply to intrigue, or even to terrorize, the
reader. Above all, he writes in order to revive at the literary
level a popular oral tradition in danger of becoming extinct.

Thus when he deals with the occult, Seignolle portrays
the Devil as he still survives in many rustic legends of France.

[2] *Le Folklore du Hurepoix.*
[3] *Le Rond des sorciers.*
[4] *Le Bahut noir.*

No need for bloodcurdling or gruesome settings: the author incarnates Satan as an entity sharing many human traits, and this anthropomorphism reflects the essence of today's French folklore—simplicity and ruggedness within the ever-present influence of nature. Following the path of Giono and Bosco, Seignolle revitalizes a wealth of popular legends. The rusticity of this folklore, however, does not entail what is still too frequently scorned as peasants' incredulity and backwardness. Where Georges Bernanos depicted the Devil as conforming to Catholic traditions (a spirit who, summoned by Mouchette, "appeared instantly, without any commotion or tumult, frighteningly quiet and self-assured"),[5] Seignolle portrays an evil spirit of popular inspiration—a man playing the role of a blacksmith in a small and remote village. This Satan repudiates his designs when he falls in love with a beautiful but mentally retarded young woman, the village idiot, who is the only one capable of recognizing his true identity. And when she is murdered by the villagers, the Devil is brought to identify himself with human suffering, transcending both his human disguise and his cosmic diabolical nature.

The works of Claude Seignolle are a true initiation into the patrimony of the rustic soul. They allow us to discover on this side of the Atlantic an author who deserves his place in the lineage of the great French storytellers. It would indeed be propitious to restore the Gothic tale to a place of prominence in the history of French literature. More than a theme or a genre, the fantastic reflects an original and privileged inspiration that still survives in the popular imagination. Through the medium of his short stories, Seignolle creates a certain nostalgia that our modern civilization is unable to eradicate.

Eric H. Deudon

[5] *Sous le soleil de Satan* (Paris: Plon, 1926), p. 221, translated from the French.

The Nightcharmer and Other Tales of Claude Seignolle

The Nightcharmer

MY old friend Dr. M. of Chateauroux had advised me to visit the manor of Guernipin, between Mazière and Rosnay, provided however that its proprietor, whose temper was often quite unpredictable, would extend an invitation to me.

It was thus that I discovered Guernipin and Geoffroy de la Tibaldière, an eccentric zoologist and bachelor, fortunately without relatives, who had sacrificed his comfort for an exceptional collection of animals, stuffed, mounted, or placed beneath bell jars. He lived in a narrow alcove where he slept on a simple cot, each of the other twenty comfortable rooms being, by his preference, crammed with dusty and docile fauna. He welcomed me graciously into his specimen-rooms, confessing to me that an unshakable collector's fever had taken hold in his tender youth. He had caught it unwittingly at the age of eight, as he playfully trapped inside empty matchboxes the meandering insectia of the Guernipin estate. Admirable little coffins, carefully labeled, once gleaming but now withered by time like the skin of their curator.

M. de la Tibaldière was a quick old man of eighty-five and himself something of a collector's piece. Guided by his expertise, I was invited to proceed meticulously through the mess of feathers, hair, and scales.

That first afternoon we saw only the first-floor rooms, and in the deepening twilight, drawing like a curtain over these local and exotic marvels, I was left with a craving to see

Originally published as "Le Hupeur," in Claude Seignolle, *Les Chevaux de la nuit et autres récits cruels*, Verviers (Belgium): Gérard, 1967
© 1967 by Claude Seignolle

more of it. Having acquired a taste for this safe and effortless hunt, I did not know just how to convey to him my desire to see all there was.

He prolonged my fervor by inviting me to stay the night there in an old high-poster bed in a rustic room he had fixed in the garret of the manor. We dined informally in the kitchen, where we were able to search through his rich memory while eating chanterelle omelettes and truffled foie gras. His servant, Sylvain, saw that our glasses were kept full to the proper level with a manorial Reuilly wine. M. de la Tibaldière being quite talkative, I looked after the proper satisfaction of his imperious enthusiasm.

The bouquet of the Reuilly enhanced the flavor of the chanterelles, brightened that of the truffles, and, indeed, quickened the already brisk tongue of my host. At midnight, lethargically spelled out by a pot-bellied clock, he was still talking, his back to the fire, as we were served by Sylvain. A man in his fifties, sunburnt to the shock of his tousled hair, Sylvain looked like an old Moorish woman (a common likeness in this part of Berry, close to Poitou, where the Saracen occupation had left its contamination).

M. de la Tibaldière evoked memories of his remote and adventurous hunts, back in the days when a rifle-sight wouldn't tremble before his eyes. Lovingly he lingered, retracing for me the time of his youth in these parts, his patient explorations of burrows, nests, and lairs. He glorified the effervescent life of the boggy soil, a paradise for its sedentary and migratory fauna. At one in the morning my head throbbed with a new knowledge of ornithology—wild duck (*Anas platychyrha*), field crow (*Chaublasmus stepera*), cheldrake (I spare you the Latin), pochard, heron, coot, wheatear, rail (*Rallus aquaticus*, it is not that I have forgotten), all scrupulously introduced. Appearance, calls, habits, and still much more.

Sylvain was slouched over an oak bench, drawn near the hearth, and as patient as a dog certain of the scraps to come, he yawned in faithfulness. As for me, despite the strain of

the long day I dared not break in on my host, so generous
with his welcome and his conversation. Still I hoped that it
would not be long before he too began to doze. But now he
had begun to go on about the mythical creatures that the
people of Brenne, dreadfully superstitious, grant to the
nights there. He told me of the Nightcharmer.

My curiosity piqued, I straightened up: the Nightcharmer! Tired as I was, I was indeed in the mood for a look
into legends. Hearing that name, Sylvain had slid across his
bench and drawn closer to the fire as if to move farther away
from us. He stared fixedly at the crackling embers as though
he were seeing them for the first time. "You should know,"
my host informed me with dogmatic assurance, "that in the
old days the family of that bird had spread so far that every
swamp in France, and often beyond, was filled with its beck-
oning spirit, a cunning, winged creature that lured the
simple-minded to utter terror."

I nodded as he proceeded in a brilliant enumeration:
the Woodcharmer of Normandy, the Nightcaller of Ar-
dennes, the Blackcaller of Brittany, the Hoowing of Limou-
sin, protean beings born of the popular imagination and
kept alive during long, troubled nights by credulous peasants. Locally, they had their Nightcharmer, the only one alive
in the region and doubtless the last remaining anywhere.

My host then aimed an imaginary rifle, and raising his
voice, threatened, "I never caught sight of the thing, otherwise I'd have . . ." and he mischievously winked at me with a
skeptic's eye before addressing his servant sympathetically,
"Is that not so, Sylvain?" But failing for once in his obedience, the man did not answer.

At last I was released. My host stood up and entrusted
me to his servant, giving him orders to see that I was well
attended. He then dismissed us with an abrupt about-face,
enviably agile. Sylvain took a pitcher of water and a lamp,
and proceeding ahead, slowly led me without looking back
through long corridors and steep stairways up to my garret
room.

I was not as disappointed as I had expected. Quite the contrary, though sultry from the heat absorbed by the roof, it was clean and pleasant. The place was large as well, with magnificent varnished beams that gleamed as we passed under them. The poster bed, made of walnut, smelled of wax. As I lifted the sheets, somewhat coarse, they exuded a fragrance of lavender. As for the four bouquets of flowered cretonne tied to the posts, if I feared there might be spiders hiding in them, my mind was set to rest as I assured myself that they would certainly be pinned, labeled after their species, and therefore prisoners and harmless. Recognizing my fears, Sylvain promptly unfolded one of them and shook the fabric to show me that no spiders lived there. And for the first time, he consented to smile at me. The weight of M. de la Tibaldière's authority now lifting, it seemed he wished to talk a bit.

And he did so as he kindly directed me around, finding for me the wash stand as well as a small round window, a source of fresh air, which he hastened to open. As I remarked that this slight opening might be insufficient, he motioned to me to follow him to a door that he unlocked and pushed open. We climbed narrow stone steps from which we emerged onto the balcony of a crenelated tower, which I had not noticed when I arrived that day at Guernipin. The view around us was prodigious. Everywhere, from beneath us to far in the distance, there was water: pools, lakes, glittering under the full moon, giving the impression of being limitlessly strung together. Framed by a vegetation that seemed thicker under the shadowy illumination, but which was, in fact, composed of sparse shrubs, the water world of Brenne appeared like a jewel, discarded for a flaw and exiled in this forgotten hole within the rich Berry.

I felt that Sylvain took great pride in offering me this surprise, and not hiding my feelings, I begged for details. The man knew his Brenne by heart. I soon knew the name of each of these mirrors, of each moor and slough. The nearest of them lay close enough to touch, a miserable morass in the process of hardening, though still treacherous to the imprudent: Oxswallow Swamp.

Now far from any wish to sleep and thereby leave this seductive nocturnal landscape, from which only a touch of life was missing, I said to Sylvain, "What a pity this celebrated Nightcharmer is only a legend, otherwise I might have heard him and applauded him enthusiastically." The servant then abruptly grabbed my arm and squeezed it. I saw that my words had quite suddenly caused him to lose his inspiration. His voice dropped and nearly vanished.

"Never wish it, sir," he whispered, "especially on a night like this. It is just the sort of night he chooses to call one of us to his death." He then persuaded me to leave the place. Back in the garret, he carefully closed and locked the tower door; in the light I looked with astonishment on his disconcerted and lightly perspiring face, a face so troubled that for an instant I felt like relieving him with a consoling slap. Still fascinated, though set in my disbelief, I tried to be cleverer in regaining his trust. I succeeded in having him sit down with me on the edge of the bed where, uniting the tone of my inquiry with that of his restlessness, I obtained some details about this formidable bird.

And so I learned that the one of which M. de la Tibaldière had spoken did indeed exist. Better yet, that his preferred abode was the Oxswallow Swamp, scarcely one-half mile from us and an equal distance from the village. He had no fearful appearance, might be any common fowl, and in fact, to better beguile his victims, could change species at will. His call, it seemed, had one too many notes . . . something slightly strident. It was his curse. To listen to it was to lose one's will to his. In numb obedience, one rose from bed, left the security of the house, and like a sleepwalker, still in nightclothes, plodded on toward this hellish creature, who already was rejoicing in his fresh new prey. As one walked on, though ankle-deep in the thick mud, one was unaware of the surrounding swamp. The bird would move back and back, further luring its victim without remorse down into the depth of the slime. Pessaut, Guérin, the old charwoman Marguerite, and many more had been lost this way, their bodies never found. All that remained were their footprints on the harder banks of the Oxswallow, which doubtless had shared the flesh with the Nightcharmer.

His call was unmistakable, alone in the night when other birds neither sung nor whistled. His first cry was a signal to rush to lock and bolt the door, barricade everywhere, clamp one's fists over one's ears, burrow in under the sheets, and above all, not leave the presence of at least one companion, so that the one might prevent the other from following the baneful wail.

Having unladen all of this on me, as one gets rid of a burdensome secret, Sylvain quickly departed, taking the lamp and leaving me to the darkness. I heard him double-lock the door, no doubt by force of habit, then descend the stairs, stumbling in his haste.

The silver needle of moon, piercing through the open window, sinking into the dark of the attic, failed to break the oppressive silence now swelling like a balloon. I undressed and lay down on the bed, forgetting in my weariness the disturbing images left me by this superstitious servant.

The heat prevented me from going immediately off to sleep. I tossed and rolled continuously until at some point I decided to open the tower door; after much groping about, I found it. The fresh breeze coming in, stirring with the air from the window, relieved me; I went back to bed. This time sleep obeyed me almost instantly.

I dreamt a dream, though at first quite pleasant, which gradually invaded me with a strange uneasiness. I found myself in an enormous ballroom where everything suggested another era, and where, relaxed and content, I sank into an armchair. A beautiful young woman, employing the most charming smiles, came to issue me an invitation . . . Impolitely, I refused her, remaining seated when I should have stood and granted her the dance. Appearing to be not the least bit shocked by my behavior, she began to laugh in the queerest manner. Her laughter seemed composed of three sharp notes, balanced with silences that completed a rhythm. Taking me by the hand, she pulled me toward her . . . I resisted . . . But her gentle strength slowly managed to lift me. Standing now, I felt naked. A sudden embarrassment forced me to run away . . . In my clumsiness I struck a wall . . . or perhaps a door . . . I couldn't remember which. I fell and people came to pick me up. They must have pitied me. Their hands supported me and carried me away . . . away from the ballroom, to a cool park and the smell of freshly cut grass. They led me to a well, and there, playfully or maliciously, I was pushed, forced to step up to and nearly over its edge.

I resisted, falling backward to the ground. Seized by a sudden terror, I tried to make myself heavy, refusing to go on with this utterly stupid act . . . I heard again the shrill laughter of the young woman, now invisible, to whom I desperately directed all my attention, regretting too late that I had not joined her.

I was awakened by the early morning chill. I found myself on the tower roof, lying shivering on the bare stone. A gray fog covered Guernipin, gradually gilded by the rising sun. The moment of astonishment over, I understood the reasons for my being in that place. There was no possible doubt: choking in the hot attic chamber and craving fresh air, I had gone up, half-conscious, to sleep in the open night. Then, leaning over a crenel, I discovered the awesome, precipitous height of the tower; and overwhelmed, I now realized what a terrible fall I had escaped!

This new day in the company of M. de la Tibaldière was passed as warmly as the one before it. I shared his vast knowledge—the enigma of the onager, the cyclical migrations of the wild African boar. Always there were anecdotes and biological digressions to assure his authority. We lunched in the park, in the cool shade of a cedar, which the wind, lightly springing up, tried in vain to ruffle. Our table was a long stone slab, taken from the earth of a nearby abbey. We ate heartily over the belly of an austere abbot, stiffly engraved there.

As we came into the evening, we had not yet reached the

second floor, where, according to my host, now suddenly excited at the thought, reposed the jewels of his collection: coelacanths, great saurians from Borneo, and other survivors from antediluvian times. And so I dined again at Guernipin, though this time I was spared the lecture following the meal. By now I had become familiar with the place and so went up to bed on my own, keeping the lamp. Fearing another awakening on the balcony, I tightly locked the door leading to the corridor. I lay down and began to read a book, but as I reached the third page it slipped from my hands; I blew out the lamp and sleep overtook me.

This second night I was not troubled by the heat—quite the contrary. Again I was caught up in a dream; again soft in its beginning . . . I was visiting Guernipin alone, discovering for myself new rooms, astonishing in their variety . . . At last I could touch and hold as I pleased birds with soft, downy plumage . . . mysterious birds in unfamiliar forms who, as I handled them, came to life and fluttered . . . Soon they were so numerous that in bumping into me, they had managed to nudge and guide me toward the freedom of the park, where they continued to surround me, flitting silently . . . M. de la Tibaldière suddenly appeared on the perron, indignantly shouting for me to return before the most secret pieces of his aviary escaped forever. Strangled by anger, his screams were like the groaning of a great bullfrog . . . Ignoring him, I suddenly fled with the heart of this unleashed flock, whose will I obeyed and with whom I was breathlessly carried away . . . I ran on until I sensed an odd oppression . . . Scarcely a breath left in me, I felt my running gradually impeded by a clammy, sticky force . . . a force that suddenly awoke me.

Today, it seems an impossible task to describe the violent repulsion I felt as I suffered under this cold viscosity. Brutally, I had been thrown back into reality, my legs deep in the slimy mud. Where was the bed on which I thought I had been sleeping? Where was Guernipin? Indeed, where was I?

Trapped by an enormous leech that slowly drew me down, I sank further into the infection of a nauseous swamp.

My hands and arms searched in vain for some solid support: a root or branch, life . . . Then a sudden bellowing like that of an angered bull stopped short my struggling. From within the marsh where I was sinking it came, loudly cutting through the darkness. Despite my terror, I was able to distinguish the call of a heron; but in place of the normal three consecutive notes, his calls were oddly disordered.

I saw him . . . violently struggling only a few feet from me. At once Sylvain's accounts came back to me. I thought of the Nightcharmer. It could only be he, shaking in his righteous laughter at his ridiculous and pathetic victim. I was, in coldest fact, within the Oxswallow.

But then I noticed that he was hopping, beating his wings as though the ooze was trying to trap and engulf him also. Seeing my redoubled straining as I fought to save myself from this mire that slowly lapped about my form, he quickened his calls as though to urge me on, as though to help me in my efforts to escape. Finally I reached a patch of grass, and setting myself free from the hungry earth, I crawled up on it. The heron had drawn closer, and spurring me on with his flapping, he helped me toward the firm soil of a pebbly path. And if, exhausted, I did not collapse there, it was by the grace of this providential bird, whose pecking had forced me to get up again and return, without the loss of another moment, towards Guernipin, which at last I could see, massive and reassuring, at hope's reach.

But it was in that instant that once more I felt that invisible and threatening force. Shackled with terror, I had a desperate feeling that a huge but impalpable single wing was flying about me like a lissome ray of nothingness in the ocean of the night. An amorphous reality was drawing me with merciless constancy back into the swamp. Without the frenzied calls of the heron, giving himself up to a paroxysmal panic, coming once more to my rescue, forcing me to flee, I admit I could not have held out against this thing that was carrying me back with it.

And at once I understood! I understood that the Nightcharmer, be it an owl, a crow, a heron, or any bird that could feel this flying death, was neither legend nor man's enemy, but rather a protector. He warned of the inexpressible peril only he could sense . . . His calls, far from ominous, were in fact an immediate alarm: himself menaced and afraid, he cried out, not so much from fear as against it. And the Ox-swallow, a propitious and putrid haven, sheltered still, after thousands of years, an invisible and insatiable monster, a sur-vivor of the times when accursed powers reigned under the subtlest forms.

But now I thought I saw two greenish glimmers . . . an illusion? A reflection of my fears? No, these were eyes! Screaming in repulsion, I wrenched myself free from this horror that had chosen me and had vainly come for me the night before . . .

In the morning M. de la Tibaldière, eager to have me visit the rooms of prehistoric ancestors, ordered his servant to go up and awaken me. But except for scattered traces of mud, Sylvain found only this note, doubtless to remain an enigma:

Never harm the Nightcharmer

A Dog Story

IT was October, 1939. The French army was scrambling and burrowing, trenching and sapping, following the example of the last Great War. We fought by ruse—ruse for food, ruse for sleep, ruse for hope. To us this was no Phony War; we had sunk our feet in it. Khaki foxes, we faced an invisible lumbering pack of green wolves who, squatting only a few kilometers away, took the war in deadly earnest.

Each day it rained more unbearably. The sky, dying of an early autumn, was wretched and depressing. Though the end of the world seemed near, we voraciously devoured these wasted years under the patronage of a benevolent field-kitchen. Sheltered beneath a humble awning, it was the heart of the detachment, the High Altar of the Holy Feeding.

And as in the distant past when the faithful erected their miserable and parasitic abodes on the hillsides of sacred shrines, and as swallows fix their wartlike nests to the fronts of houses, the detachment had erected its tents and parked its trucks in the orbit of the field-kitchen so that, at any given moment, we might become drunken with the nourishing scents of beef stew, fried potatoes, rice and gravy . . . or the ritual coffee. These were precious consolations artfully cooked by Léon, my accomplice. I was at the time his food-supply clerk.

I must say something more about the field-kitchen. Looking like a great toad, it had two plump bellies that were

Originally published as "Le Chien pourri," in Claude Seignolle, *Les Chevaux de la nuit et autres récits cruels*, Verviers (Belgium): Gérard, 1967 © 1967 by Claude Seignolle the front lockers for meats and vegetables, and a bladder, the sacred little coffee tank in the rear, at the bottom of which one would inevitably find, during the monthly scouring, the skins and tiny bones of overcooked rats who had inexpertly fallen in, coffee filchers having left the lid ajar.

The hearths were huge and solid, and fortunately so, since to light the wet, green wood we were forced to douse it with gasoline, ten or twenty gallons lighted by the toss of a torch from a safe distance. Without fail the fire would ignite and rage, each time projecting out from the hearth a comet's tail, which threatened to kick back like an old siege cannon. The dumping area, the open wound of any field-kitchen, lay a little to one side. In a week's time we would pour a half-dozen drums of gas on its rottenness, purifying it of the worms that swarmed there in millions and overflowed onto the surrounding mud, in close columns wandering aimlessly; disoriented larvae, the strongest of which pushed back the weakest, reserving for themselves the best places on the tiers of repeatedly renewed garbage. We would empty three or four cans, strike a match, and as it burned we could hear the hideous sizzling and popping of bursting worms. Afterwards, it seemed as many remained. It was an unimaginable sight: a putrid, swarming mass, a good ten inches thick, undulating and swelling like a breathing chest.

And there were dogs—errant and hungry. Miserable German shepherds that had lost both their kennels and their masters, who themselves had lost their farms and their property when summoned to leave immediately for the frontier zone of the Maginot Line. And there we were with all these strays scratching around our feet.

They were the lost dogs of the lost villages, wandering about our camp, some frightened, some vicious, all emaciated. One among them, with neither god nor devil to follow—man will always be a god or a devil to his dog according to the tenor of his stroking—used to come each day, sniffing the heap of trash, and having made his selection, would abruptly snatch away a bone on which remained some putrifying flesh.

He was a chilling sight with his crusty sores, his coat eaten away by mange, and his skin oozing a continuous infection that drew black blood and over which mud daubed its fragile armor of earth. What remained of his withered ear dangled half-eaten away by the same disease that was stripping the flesh from his chops. And worse, he dragged along a generously gangrened leg, snapped no doubt under the wheel of a truck. Though he was little more than a disgusting thing, a bag of pus procreated by a charnel house more contaminated than our dumping area, he moved our hearts to pity, this rotting dog, and did so with a pleading glance that could move the most hardened of us, truck drivers for the most part, who had each run down a half-dozen dogs and cats, not counting a string of hens and perhaps even an occasional reckless pedestrian. His eyes were the only purity that survived in this animal horror.

"It's a spaniel," said Léon when he first saw it.

"Was," I corrected him.

We tolerated him around us until one day it became too much. Having wallowed in the heap, he fell asleep on it and very nearly killed what remained of our precious appetites.

And so Léon and I decided we would do him in, though it was not at all easy; we lost courage when, having cornered him in a grassy hole, we began to club him with blows as violent as they were clumsy; the wretched animal cried out like a child punished for mischief he hadn't made. It was as if we were killing something human; and yet, it was for him, so that he would no longer suffer and his agony could finally come to an end. Of course we could have poisoned him, but after having swallowed such foul waste in such great quantities, what poisons were there against which he wouldn't be immune? Or we could have shot him, but the order was strict and categorical, and disobeying it might have brought upon us the same fate: not a shot to be fired. Save bullets. Damn it all! We were at war: war against the mud, war against the worms, war against the dogs.

The poor animal was wriggling and howling beyond madness in that hole where we tortured him like cowards with our bludgeoning; each time we hit him we jumped aside in fear that his pus-swollen body might burst and drown us in a great gush of bacteria.

"We've got to crush his head," raged Léon.

But that was the hardest place to hit, not because the dog in his struggling was able to dodge our blows, but because all we saw of him were his imploring eyes, begging for mercy, eyes that could neither believe nor comprehend that it was we who were his torturers. Then, looking away, with blind strikes we broke his skull and the animal moved no more, dead at last; throwing our contaminated bludgeons far away, we covered the hole with heavy stones.

That night, as I lay under the truck on the thick straw under which rats moved freely, I was still nauseated. Drowsy as I was, I knew only too well that I could not soon fall asleep. Léon was snoring. He had drunk himself to sleep, trying to forget.

It was then that I heard it: it came as an odd crackling of leaves, and a little later, after a bit of fitful sleep, I noticed a lapping sound from a short distance; a fetid odor floated around me. I sat up, my hand grabbed the flashlight, and I flicked it on.

My God! There before me stood that decaying dog. And

now, among his old sores, he bore fresh ones where drying blood had mixed with black dirt: the very wounds opened by our bludgeons. His pink tongue, the only bit of pure flesh that remained to him, dangled and panted; he sniffed around, found a dab of rice in the bottom of a can, and made a meal of it.

A mute terror drove me to my knees as I retreated toward the hollow where Léon slept. I shook him. He awoke in a fury, ready to kick out at me. "Look! . . . for God's sake, look!" I shouted, with sickly spasms in my voice. Then, like two madmen, we grabbed our rifles and fired all our forbidden bullets into this monstrous spectre from beyond a dog's grave.

And at last, for a second time and forever, he passed away, the rotting dog from some obscure place, a beast whom hunger had revived.

The Healer

GLAUDE MICHEL, a gardener from the town of Coulon-delles, had all the plumpness and gentleness that some women look for in a husband. He was a man with whom a peaceful and happy married life could be confidently shared. With his big round face gleaming with generosity and his paunchy fifty-year-old looks, Glaude was kindness itself, offered to anyone who wanted it.

Glaude was also a sort of countryside conjuror. But he was quite different from those common faith healers, those quacks with their easy tricks who could be found most anywhere in every village, like so many bonesetters, medicine men, and other assorted charlatans. No, from birth he had inherited from his ancestors a most uncommon gift: he was endowed with the power of putting ailments to "sleep." So if your chest had absorbed an icy cold, caught at nightfall by the river; if a chill was pressing its big thumbs against your lungs, so strongly that you would feel them with each breath, what could you do? There were only two possible choices: you could either bury yourself under three layers of blankets after drinking a quart of hot sugared wine, or you could go and see Glaude, bent over his flowers, and ask for his help.

Quietly twirling his white mustache, which looked like a carnation under his nose, he would closely listen to the sounds of your breathing. Then he would sniff the sweat on your brow and finally poke his hand under your shirt, where

Originally published as "Le Dormeur," in Claude Seignolle, *Contes de Sologne*, Paris: Éditions de Sologne, 1969
© 1969 by Claude Seignolle

the congestion was burning you. "You in pain?" he would ask, slightly wary. That's when you had to lie. You had to hide the pain, even if it showed itself in your eyes. For as he grew older Glaude was less and less willing to "sleep" pains. Long ago he had cured burning colics, because then his bowels were like the copper pipes of a still, able to turn fire into water. But as time went on he had put up so much resistance against the shocks of so many ailments that parts of his body had grown weaker. His bones were no longer encased in iron. The hard leather of his joints had worn off, and alcohol no longer ran in his veins instead of blood.

By now he would look at you suspiciously and ask, "You hurtin', I mean hurtin' real bad?" That would compel you to lie in order to reassure him. And so you would reply with something like, "It's not the pain so much, but it kind of bothers me when I raise my arms." And old Glaude would believe you, though he was never completely fooled; he was just hoping for not too big a lie. Besides, one or two more pneumonias could hardly do any damage to his lungs, since they were still roaring like two beehives. Then he would ask you for exactly three gold coins, which you had to give him without haggling. That was part of the treatment. "The Church makes you pay for a miracle . . . so why shouldn't I?" he would say as a comfort to his clients. However, if in church it was easy to cheat with an apparent generosity, promising gold while actually slipping pennies into the anonymity of an almsbox, it was impossible to fool Glaude with copper coins, for his hands knew the difference quite well. Once you had given him the money you were already cured, and your torments would be transferred to him.

Old Glaude's treatment was always successful and speedy. He would notify his wife to leave him alone on his bed. Each time she would loudly protest and cry out, shaking the wrinkles of her neck, which dangled like a turkey wattle. But then he would remind her of his warts, and showing the back of his fingers, which were full of them, he would maliciously pretend to give them all back to her. The threat worked

every time. His wife would give in, remembering with grati-
tude Glaude's promptness in "sleeping" them away—the day
she nearly lost her job at the diner—the owner's wife feeling
faint at the mere sight of dirty fingernails. Glaude had transferred them onto himself in thirty-six hours of uninter-
rupted sleep. And so his wife would sigh with resignation,
thinking of the time she would spend alone while her husband slept for days. Who knows? It could even take a week,
like the time he had "slept" away the malignant fever of
the pharmacist's younger daughter. After that experience
Glaude had sworn never to invite that kind of disease into
him again: it had cost him twenty pounds of good fat.

If the miseries that afflicted others still continued to
graft themselves onto him, as he soothed and digested them
with the power of his body, it was evident that as he grew
older they stayed with him longer and longer. Like his wife's
warts, Gravier's arthritis was still in Glaude's body, grinding
his bones. Sometimes this ingrate would even make fun of
Glaude, ironically asking news of "his" twinges. But Glaude
would scare the teaser, pretending to give him back his pains,
right then and there.

One evening a man from Chicrolles, the nearby village,
came to see Glaude at the bar, where he was enthusiastically
engaged in a game of dominoes. The man managed to take
him outside and described his ailment, stammering so much
that the gardener had to make him repeat his story several
times. It looked as though his prospective patient wasn't
quite right in the head. Now old Glaude was willing to "sleep"
back pains and heartburns, but mental problems were definitely out of the question. Just as he would never accept to
"sleep" a potentially fatal disease. After all, how would he
ever get rid of it?

The stranger was a fidgety, skinny character with feverish eyes. His face was not a pleasant sight to see, and his fearful looks only added to the aura of sickness he radiated. The
gardener began to wonder if he'd had a drink or two too

many and was seeing things. However, reassured as the man managed to compose himself, he figured the stranger was probably only scared that somebody might try to explain some of his absences from home. Glaude was now satisfied that the man wasn't crazy but was only panicking, probably terrorized by a shrew of a wife. Knowing that he was himself quite levelheaded about such things, and seeing this man literally out of his senses, the healer sympathetically agreed to help him. All this trifling nervousness was going to be "slept" in a few hours. Afterwards, it would be nothing more than a memory.

The stranger left without even giving his name, but he turned out to be quite generous, putting a handful of gold coins in the gardener's hand. There were so many that Glaude had to run after him to give them back. He would keep only three coins. More than that was of no use for this cure, which wasn't even worth that much.

That night Glaude went to sleep early to take upon himself the stranger's ailment. But this time he was troubled as never before. Usually he would "doze off" a muscle ache and feel a pull on his joints. Or if he had agreed to cure a high fever, he would shiver in a cold sweat; a good pneumonia would smolder like fire in his lungs. This time, however, he felt no pain at all. Instead something much worse happened: he was invaded with desires that would make the Devil himself blush. He was eyeing little girls as they left from school, and he felt overwhelmed with itches in his groin . . . Soon he was following the prettiest one, hiding from her with all the ruse of desire. He jumped on her as she walked by the thick woods. He dragged her by her blouse and it tore open, revealing the white skin of her back, which almost made him faint with excitement. He tried to kiss her, but the young girl resisted. She screamed and rolled with him on the ferns. Her skirt lifted, uncovering the top of her thighs. Instead of being afraid of getting caught, Glaude felt his desire grow in him as he tore off the girl's clothes, throwing himself upon this struggling body that could do nothing against his crazed strength . . . He crushed her under his weight . . . She scratched his face but it didn't hurt him at all, it only added to his pleasure . . . But she went on screaming louder and louder, so much so that to force her to quiet down, he grabbed her throat and strangled her like a chicken.

And he dreamed it all again, endlessly consummating the rape and starting it all over with another girl. He tossed in his bed, moaning with such desire that his wife became alarmed by the flow of obscenities that he was shouting. She finally dared enter the bedroom and tried to awaken him from his torments; but if she hadn't backed off just in time, he would have dragged her onto his bed.

When he awoke Glaude realized that he had accepted a satanic proposition, and he was wise enough to decide to break it off, despite the bestial pleasure he had just experienced. A long time ago, while "sleeping" a hatred he had taken to be just a mild anger, he had gotten up in his sleep, loaded his shotgun, and left his house to go and kill the mayor, who was actually the prey of his patient. Without the winter cold that clutched him in his nightgown and woke him in the garden, Glaude would have become an assassin. Fortunately, he had been able to break the arrangement by immediately returning the three gold coins that had sealed the deal. His patient was not at home, but Glaude had left the money in an obvious spot, on a white sheet of paper on the kitchen table. Returning to his house and seeing the gold coins, his patient had wondered whether they had fallen out of the sky. He had touched them with the tips of his fingers, and that had been enough to cancel the deal and allow his hatred to go back into him. This time, too, Glaude would have to act fast and in the same manner with the stranger.

His legs still numb with sleep and his senses slightly dulled, Glaude took the road to Chicrolles to find the stranger and call off the deal. He looked for him everywhere, not daring to ask anyone. He searched all the shops and bars with a surprising boldness, for ordinarily he never bothered people in the slightest. All the streets and alleys saw him walk by at

least two or three times. So did the fields, for the stranger
was not easy to find. And every time Glaude passed by the
high school, even going back there on purpose, he would
slow down and listen. Now he would have really liked to hear
the girls sing, whereas before he had always been annoyed by
the schoolgirls of Coulondelles. But this studious silence worried him, making him fear that perhaps they had already left
. . . When suddenly the doors opened, as the teachers let the
whole flock out for recess. And he saw them, fresh and play-
ful, shouting and running after each other, teasing the boys
or quietly talking to each other.

Glaude was struck by such a shower of desire that he felt
dizzy and had to grab the iron gate with both hands, looking
like a man drunk on a gallon of cheap wine. But then, feeling
guilty and scared that one of the young girls might recognize
him, he rushed to hide behind one of the basswood trees on
the square, where he continued eyeing the one he had already chosen. He had to admit it was only gossip to say that
people were thin-blooded in Chicrolles. Here the girls were
full of life . . . But after all, what did he care about these,
since he could have others at Coulondelles, as many as he desired . . . Yet Glaude managed to shake off this tormenting
obsession and was ashamed to find himself burning alive
with these lewd thoughts. For though they were not his own,
they were gradually creeping up on him. Finally he made up
his mind and walked inside the city hall to inquire at the re-
ception desk. The employee was at first pleasant, but a funny
look crossed his face when Glaude described the stranger
to him.

"You wouldn't be looking for Louis, by any chance?" he
asked in a disgusted tone of voice.

"I'm telling you," repeated the gardener, "I don't know
his name, otherwise I wouldn't be here asking you. All I
know is that he wears a dirty beige corduroy jacket."

The clerk looked at Glaude suspiciously and replied,
"That's Louis for sure, what do you want with him?"

"I want to give him back some cash he loaned me," answered Glaude.

"In that case, you're that much richer," said the clerk, trying to muster a smile.

"Damn it, man, why?" shouted Glaude, feeling more and more uneasy in front of this man.

"Because," the clerk bluntly replied as he grabbed his throat with his hands, "because that son of a bitch hanged himself yesterday after raping Lucette Richard, and he's probably the one who strangled Lantier's daughter a month ago. You can bet he would have raped others if guilt hadn't put a rope around his neck."

Suddenly understanding that the stranger's vice was in his groin forever, and that he had no more rival in this vicious hunt, the gardener dropped into a chair. And in front of the stupefied clerk, he started to cry hysterically at his newfound potency.

Starfish

SHE arrived alone, driving a luxurious limousine. The caretaker had been impatiently awaiting her, standing in the gray haze of this December dusk. The winter wind was howling angrily at this small village by the sea, a town now deserted and abandoned, the way a resort looks in the off-season. She rolled down the window and told him her name. Her voice was gentle and pleasant, but he heard it edged with silent sorrow; she apologized for being late. Troubled and reluctantly friendly, the caretaker answered that waiting was part of his job; he was used to it and didn't mind at all. He hastened to open the car door, but as he saw her stepping out, his impatience turned into apprehensiveness.

She wore dark suede boots and was wrapped in a rich fur coat whose hood covered her head. Her face was almost entirely hidden behind a black shawl, and her eyes, compulsively staring into the distance, were the only features that could be seen. The caretaker tried to look as natural as possible. He knew that the people who rented this gigantic villa in the winter wished to be left alone, as if they were hiding a suspicious need for isolation. Yet he sensed that somehow this woman had to have worse reasons than all the others. She had brought only an expensive leather suitcase, but as he picked it up it felt empty, and that added another measure of distrust to his already suspicious disposition.

In the hall he flicked on the light, but a sudden short cir-

Originally published as "Le Miroir," in Claude Seignolle, *Contes Fantastiques de Bretagne*, Paris: G. P. Maisonneuve et Larose, 1969
© 1969 by Claude Seignolle

cuit finished off the brief glow of the chandelier. He cursed
in the dark, found his lighter, and went groping down to the
basement. But it was useless. The lights would not come back
on; the lingering humidity of the house had once more defeated the fuse box. "I'll have to call the electrician," he
grumbled as he walked back upstairs. Despite its temporary
annoyance, the blackout had given him a welcome opportunity to leave the woman for a moment. And though the
basement was dark and damp, he found it more cheerful
than the invading silence of the stranger. Lighting a candle, he rushed through the showing of the first floor, even
though it had always been his pleasure to initiate the new-
comers to the splendor of more than a dozen rooms. He took
her suitcase and climbed the stairs leading to the master bedroom. The stranger followed him, seemingly distant in her
halo of despair, but still much too close for his comfort.

He opened the door and came into the room, which was
basking in the glow of a sleepy hearth. He quickly revived the
fire, prodding it with a poker. The embers crackled and came
back to life as he covered them with new logs. Left to their
hunger the flames rose and snorted at the cinders, projecting
around the room the anger of their stirred-up brightness.
"The fire will give you some light for the time being . . . The
bed is made . . . If you need another blanket . . ." the caretaker went on, trying his best to fend off the growing uneasiness that the woman radiated. He felt as though she were
one of those frighteningly beautiful and exotic flowers that
emanate a beguiling and deceitful scent, the better to paralyze
those who would dare approach her. So he half-heartedly
praised the excitement that animated the house in the sum-
mertime. "It's a house for young people . . . You should see it
during the holidays . . . Hear the children laugh and play . . .
And all the disguises . . . and the Carnival of course . . . This
place don't like winters . . . It sure don't!" Meanwhile the
stranger had sat on the edge of the bed, staring at the flames.
Was she listening to him at all? He sensed that she was not.
He placed a candle on the table and hurried out of the room,
closing the door behind him.

The woman's shadow suddenly arched on the wall. She gave way to a gentle sobbing while her fingers brushed her bandaged face, in the manner of someone who would hesitate to caress somebody else's face. She slowly followed her chin line, lingered on her cheeks, and avoided touching her nose and ears, as though they were fragile. Ever since she had left the hospital, after a dreadful car accident, she felt as if she had been wearing a hideous mask, a living veil molded with uneven strips of grafted flesh taken from her body and pieced, welded together, to allow her new face to be born. "They told me my features would live again . . . They swore I would look just like before . . . just like before!" The haunting litany resounded in her head. She got up, went to the window, and opened it. The wind rushed in and started to peel off the small and thin pages of a calendar that had been left on the wall a few months before. And now the wind was catching up with time, ready to erase the entire span of a human life, were it only given the chance.

"They have frozen my lips . . . Sewn my cheeks and my nose . . . I can feel it . . . They have turned me into living death. Forced me to run away from myself . . . To run away in vain from this other face that will soon be mine!" But there she was, alone and yet so crowded in this room, she, the famous actress, the embodiment of the most exquisite charms; the sun of millions of fans who, at this very moment all around the world, were enraptured by the grace of her body and infatuated with the incomparable beauty of her face. She had come to hide here, in this desolate place, with her new unknown self, plastered inseparably onto her flesh. And it would be a month at least before she could see her new face. One month! Time for hope, enough time to get used to the worst.

But she could wait no longer. Despite the stern warnings of her plastic surgeon, she wanted to know right then and there. She had already made up her mind on her way to the villa. Now she was away from the doctors, away from their pleas for patience, away from it all! Now she was ready for the test of truth. She stood up and looked for a mirror. She immediately found one, as though it had been waiting for her: a small mirror framed in the upper panel of an old door. Blown by a draft, the flames of the fireplace were lighting it, alternating shadows with reflections. It was just what she needed. She threw her heavy fur coat on the bed and came to the mirror. Taking the shawl off her white bandages, she revealed her third and temporary face: a helmet made of cotton, slit only by one hostile opening, which was her only tie with the outside world.

And then slowly unrolling the gauze, she began to free herself, at the risk of suffering even more. Her courage gave way when only a few strips remained. She stopped, closed her eyes as tightly as she clenched her fists, and started to bang on the mirror, on this cynical device impassively waiting to destroy her. She hit it enough to break it, but the glass held on. She did not have to unroll the rest of the bandages; they fell off by themselves, leaving her with the sensation of a nakedness she had never experienced before. Finally, she opened her eyes and saw herself.

Rather, she saw what they had done to her: a face made of sewed-up patches of discolored flesh, unevenly melted together, furrowed with deep wrinkles; a monstrous truth at which she was now staring in a daze, as if this grotesque spectacle had been the highest achievement of her acting career . . . An opaque veil of despair fell before her eyes. She turned away from the mirror, opened the door, and left the house. She walked across the loneliness of the deserted beach until her feet felt the cold caress of the sea. She gazed at the raging water and determined to make it her grave; she walked on toward the chilling embrace of the deep. It did not even frighten her. As a young girl she had almost drowned in a boating accident. And today, she felt as if she had finally returned to satisfy the frustrated hunger of the waves.

When the electrician returned with the caretaker, it took him almost an hour to restore the electricity. They then went upstairs to notify the new tenant that everything was all right, but repeated knocking yielded no reply. Intrigued, the caretaker tried turning the doorknob. The room was empty, the window wide open. They came in and turned on the light. Neither the bed nor the suitcase had been disturbed. Seeing a black shawl entangled with some kind of a long bandage on the floor, the electrician bent down to take a closer look. His curiosity satisfied, he straightened up and his eyes met the mirror.

He screamed with such terror that his companion was frozen in his tracks. In the depths of the mirror, turned back into transparent glass by the loss of its silvering, which had completely fallen off, he saw the unmistakable greenish and swollen face of a putrefied corpse—the grinning revelation of a crime hidden for several months! A few minutes later the two men tried to move the door, but the small handle was hopelessly jammed. Pushed by the courage of a morbid curiosity, they finally pried the door open with a crowbar.

A narrow closet, unknown to the caretaker, was behind it. He cautiously looked inside and his repulsion suddenly vanished. "Well, I'll be damned!" he exclaimed in a loud voice, and reaching inside without fear or disgust, he took down from a hook a tall dummy, swollen with seaweed and dressed up in mildewed clothes. The realistic paper mask that he wore like a face from another world reached exactly the height of the mirror—the memory of a time when the summer carnival had to put up with all kinds of ugliness. It fell to the floor with the lightness of a dead leaf.

At dawn, the ebb tide was forced to surrender a body from among the reefs that had reappeared on the long, colorless beach. A few shell gatherers saw it from a distance, as if it were a crucified, giant starfish. They came closer and saw that it was a svelte human star, rocked by the sea and lying face down amidst the pebbles. A fisherman ran up and freed one of her bare feet caught between the rocks. He turned her over and stretched her out on her back. All at once the women kneeled down, driven not only by the respect owed to the dead but also by the heartrending emotion that gripped them as they saw in her face an angelic beauty beyond the grace of her human body. With their hats in their hands the men stood transfixed, struck by a breathtaking feeling of divinity.

"She . . . she looks like . . ." a woman dared at last, "she looks like the one in the movies."

"Yes, maybe," someone answered in a whisper of reverence, "but this one is so much more beautiful!"

The Outlander

A last remnant of the dying year, this December day drags out its sadness. Over the woods, towards Souesnes, the edge of twilight slowly crushes down upon the horizon and storms Sologne, whose land is now clothed in a ghastly haze. The village of Brandes is still shrouded by the light mist of its bluish breath and the scent of burnt wood. In the long, muddy, and shivering street, all human life has now disappeared; everyone has returned to the cozy world of his tiny home, where everything is light, everything is warmth of the heart . . .

Meanwhile, master of the forge, Christophe swings the weight of his heavy sledgehammer. Looking like a strong oak-tree branch subdued by some sort of magic, his gnarled arm springs out of his rolled-up sleeve. His iron fist kneads the reddish and living metal, whose scorched and tamed blood gradually oozes out, leaving a grayish flesh behind. The glittering of the hearth shines out upon the skin of his arm. His muscles flutter, as though they were weasels imprisoned in a supple red leather pouch. By forging the metal, Christophe's muscles forge themselves. He whistles, so as to encourage the rhythm of his hammer, but it is not a whistle born of joyful lips; it is a song that hisses through hardworking teeth. And when Christophe stops hammering, he buries the metal back under the embers to revive it. He listens to the wheezing of the bellows, as if the echo of his

Originally published as "Le Diable en sabots," in Claude Seignolle, *Un Corbeau de toutes couleurs*, Paris: Denoël, 1962
© 1962 by Claude Seignolle

own voice were coming out of this huge, dried-up, and hollow toad, breathing through the folds of its flabby skin.

Everything is stirring around Christophe. As though they were angry, the embers burst out of the hearth, the tongs wriggle away from the cold water, and escaping from the street, the evening breeze shelters itself in the soot-covered chimney. Already pitch-dark, the night outside awaits the blacksmith's lassitude, a night that longs to see the fire die out, so that it might also glean some of the warmth of this lair. But the man is not the least bit tired. Without haste he again hoists up his hammer and molds the metal with precise blows, materializing a shape already formed in his mind. With each new stroke the anvil rings out as soundly as a huge bell. The man is in no hurry to finish. He has no desire to remove the leather apron that makes him look like one of those powerful men of long ago, before iron was even known, when they were still clothed in animal skins. As he stands up straight, Christophe looks formidable, half man, half beast, as if he would actually draw his strength from this tamed and hardened ox-skin.

He still does not feel like throwing his apron upon the anvil, thus bringing a long day of efforts to a close. He does not have the slightest wish to join his wife, who, in the nearby kitchen, has no desire either of seeing him coming home. There is no longer anything alive between them . . . Not a word, not even a gesture of friendship. After all the years that have passed by, all alike, they now suffer the torture of childless marriages. And as he works Christophe endures once again the reminder of his untold despair, and he tries in vain to break and shatter a sorrow far more unyielding than the toughest of metals. There would be no children, no tomorrows for his shop. The tools would no longer sing for Christophe, and who knows whose clumsy and unskilled hands they would obey one day? As he stands before the roaring flames of the hearth, this bitter thought gives him meandering chills. No longer able to contain a sudden burst of rage, he pounds the anvil as if he wanted to break it, but his blows are so forceful that the handle lashes out at his hand, bruising his bones and leaving him choking, as if he had gulped down a whole glass of grain alcohol . . . No children, and a shop made for one, or two, or even three sons . . . Damn it all!

After staring for a brief moment at the ravenous fire feeding on the imprisoned embers, he walks to the door and opens it. The night outside looks like a wall of nothingness, an omen of the years that lie in wait for him and through which he will have to journey in solitude, dragging along a wife more useless than a shadow. To Christophe this future looks like an immense pond of silt and ink. But fortunately, beyond all this, there would have to be an end. There is an end to everything. Patience was all he needed, but tonight Christophe realizes that he doesn't have much left. It has worn so thin that it is now within a hairbreadth of leaving him.

A shivering thought races through him, for he has just felt the presence of an invisible and dreadful seducer. And now something shatters in his head and subdues him. An irresistible power seems to control his will with the same precision that he had in handling his hammer. He now stands face to face with the seducer who, speaking to him for the first time, gives Christophe an order as piercing as if a nail were being driven through his temples. "Be done with it. Be done!" Without any will to resist it, Christophe feels himself becoming an obedient and docile instrument: a tool now destined to forge his own undoing. Crushed, and without questioning this mysterious exigency, he goes around the anvil and looks up to the massive and intertwined rafters of the ceiling. His mind is immediately made up, and as he stares at the beams his unshaven face, anointed with sweat and soot, reflects his hopelessness. His lips are searching for a song he used to know a long time ago, but he gives up. His heart refuses to bring back the past. In his defeat, Christophe would still like to brag in front of the Christophe who used to be a pillar of strength. But upon his soiled cheeks tears are now flowing, as cutting as scythe blades. As he looks back down on the floor they run into his mouth, leaving the bitter taste of his agony, forcing him on his knees, while he takes his head in his hands and abandons himself to his despair. Christophe knows that he is powerless against the hurried reaper who has come to cut him down like a mere blade of grass.

Wiping a tired hand across his eyes, he smears his tears, daubing upon his face the blackness that already inhabits his heart. He knows that such a pain coming with so much force can only be the last one a man could possibly endure. And this thought comforts him somehow and helps him through this unexpected and yet so strangely desired outcome. He struggles to his feet, goes straight to his workbench, and grabs the rope used to restrain the legs of animals about to be shod. The rope is strong, supple, and oily; some hair is stuck to it, and it emanates such a strong smell of life that Christophe inhales its essence for a moment. This pungent scent seems so distant to him that he already sees himself on the other side of this life. No hesitation of any kind will now hinder him as he walks to his death. He acts as though he were performing a simple task, just as any conscientious craftsman would.

Climbing on top of the anvil, Christophe holds out his arm towards a beam that is almost obligingly separated from the ceiling, and he slips the rope over it. As he ties the knots, they seem to him much too weak for a man of his weight, and in a brief soliloquy he murmurs these last words, "A blacksmith with my strength needs at least three knots." He ties ten of them. Five up against the beam, five down under the slipknot. When at last he passes the rope over his head, he stays still for a moment. Wearing this wreath of hemp awakens within all the compassion he had always felt at the sight of Jesus Christ on the cross, wreathed with His thorny crown. He makes the sign of the cross, not for himself, but in memory of the Lord. Then he quickly slips around his neck this assuaging choker. The smell of wool grease so overcomes him that the last reminder of his human life is an animal scent.

He hurls himself from the anvil, and the rope suddenly becomes a straight line between the beam and his body. The knots hold on. The rope vibrates, but they resist; they could have hauled the weight of a horse just as well. Wrenching itself free from his broken neck, a loud hiccup carries Christophe's soul away . . . His arms refuse to die; still writhing with life, they are frantically striking the air . . . But he quickly turns purplish-blue under the kisses that death hurriedly drops upon his face . . . Soon the veil of the dead blacksmith is swinging like a still shadow. Projected through the window by the flames of the hearth, it reaches a nearby path covered with dry leaves . . . You could almost swear that it is this shadowy double who scatters them around, while they are being dispersed by a gentle breeze skimming the ground.

Meanwhile, accompanied by the rapping of dry wood, a huge man agilely walks past the first house of the village—the house of Sabeur, the old park ranger. The man emerges from the path that opens up a wide and straight line of sand through the shrub-covered moor, only to end abruptly, no longer leading anywhere. With each step his clogs ring like wooden bells. Within them his feet go back and forth as if they were dry nuts in a shell. From the shoulders of his tall body hangs a large black cape that looks like a living patch of night, cut out from the darkness. His long strides sway his hips, and with each jostling step he looks as if his chest alone were pulling his whole frame forward. His arms thrash the air, reaping through the murk. And thus, holding onto the night, he moves on swiftly and soon finds himself in the heart of the village, as if the moor had just thrust him out, disburdening itself of a parasite. Looking like a giant bat trying to walk on two legs, the newcomer is immediately attracted by the bright lights of an inn. He goes straight to the door and opens it.

Graubois, the innkeeper, is alone in the dining room when he sees the tall black form coming in. Noticing a table already set, the stranger thereupon occupies it, as if the whole dining room belonged to him. Graubois does not dare tell him that this table is his own. He had just left it a moment ago to see what was making so much noise outside. Stiff as a poker in her drab clothes, Mrs. Graubois comes out of the kitchen bringing a plate of sausage and hot sauerkraut. She too stares at the stranger without a word, without telling him to go sit at another table. At once she is subdued by his self-assurance, the rough features of his face, and above all by the piercing look in his eyes that stabs her like a needle in the back of her neck. The Graubois are known as a braggart two-some, but the man is so imposing that their awe soon turns into hostile embarrassment. Mrs. Graubois sets her plate on another table while her husband brings knives and forks, which he has just removed from under the stranger's nose. But the latter remains seated without a word of excuse. He does not even pay attention to the woman, who looks at him, holding back her anger. How could this couple ever guess that the seeds of a collective tragedy have just been sown, and that like a hundred stalks of crawling ivy they will proliferate, soon to reach into the very soul of this village?

The innkeeper finally recovers his voice. "What would you like to drink?" he asks, while resting his hand on his wife's arm, so as to contain her growing rage. He fears that she might unleash it upon the stranger and, who knows, drag him into a brawl. "A bottle of white wine, and make it quick!" answers the man, flinging his reply at Graubois. He speaks with a strong countryside accent, and his tone is so harsh that each word rings out like an order. Mrs. Graubois swallows her anger, and for once she thinks that her husband was right to restrain her from openly insulting the stranger. She now feels that his voice could have broken her with just a few words. So she puts on an air of docility, and when her husband leaves to get a bottle of wine, she gives free rein to her imperious curiosity. "Where are you going to at this hour of the night?" she asks, mustering a smile. The man leans his back against the wall and stretches out two legs as long as rake handles. "Maybe here . . . maybe somewhere . . ." he replies evasively, without even looking at her. Each syllable seems to strike at another between his tongue and his teeth, as if he were spitting out stones. He then reaches out his hand toward a slice of bread left on the table. The inn-keeper's wife looks at his long and delicate fingers. His nails are trimmed as if he had never done any manual labor. She now thinks that he might be the schoolteacher of a nearby village, and answering the man's silence, she lets out an "Oh, I see," in a tone of conviction.

Her husband returns with a glass and a bottle and cautiously places them on the table. He then asks the same question as his wife's, and when he doesn't obtain any answer, Mrs. Graubois motions him to come and sit down in front of her. "Maybe here . . . maybe somewhere else," she repeats angrily, lingering on each word, "didn't you hear him?" "All right, all right," grumbles her husband, who sits down and starts to gulp his cold soup.

His wife nibbles at her food without chewing anything, swallowing it straight down to save her teeth, which are slowly chipping away, like the falling pieces of an old ruined wall. She swallows a mouthful of cabbage and gets an eyeful of the stranger; a piece of sausage and a glimpse of the man. She eats a little of everything, through her mouth and through her eyes. She blinks like a hen watching both the farmer's hands and the corn on the ground. But soon, with rapid and piercing glances, she no longer eats and gazes hungrily at the stranger.

He takes his time as he drinks his wine, even though he refills his glass as soon as it is empty. With each sip he looks at the door, while his sullen face seems to take on a malevolent smile. No, it must be only the play of a moving shadow, projected onto him from the lamp hanging above. But gradually anxiety is taking hold of the Graubois, who now fear that the man might have come to rob them, and so they suspiciously stare at him, as if they could somehow read his thoughts. Despite the harshness of his features, there is still an expression of youth on his lips. The stranger must be forty years old . . . perhaps less, but not more . . . His protruding face is like an ochered mask slit by two oval-shaped orbits, and the penetrating stare of his green eyes has the steadiness of an animal's gaze. The head appears elongated and out of proportion to his tall and brawny frame. A spindling nose forms a pillar that supports a forehead half-hidden behind his raven-

black hair, and the strength that exudes from his face has the cutting thrust of a plowshare, ready to tear out any will daring to oppose his own.

If at first the innkeepers think they can easily read into the stranger's face, they discover that each new glance brings out other particularities that seem to erase what they have just seen, as if his features were shaped into a dozen different facets whose amazing mobility astonishes the Graubois, as much as it disconcerts them.

His first bottle over, the man asks for another, and as Graubois comes to his table and hesitates, staring at him as if he were some kind of exotic animal, the stranger smiles for the first time. His lips tighten into a thin line, while a stunning and ruthless beauty flickers in his eyes. Graubois winces at the blow and quickly stares at the dresser, even though he knows by heart the design of each plate that it contains. The newcomer takes out of his pocket a leather purse. He casually opens it and with two fingers retrieves a freshly minted gold coin, which he throws on the table. Graubois grabs it immediately, fearing that the man might change his mind, and as he leans on the table the innkeeper sees that the purse is filled with gold coins, which glitter and wriggle in the stranger's hand. Graubois's scowling face turns to a mask of complacency. Relieved from his fears, he now needs to talk. "With that much gold, you could buy the whole town," he says, laughing. The man puts the purse back into his pocket as he dryly replies, "If there's something to buy, I'll buy it." "Well, there's always something for sale," continues Graubois, whose eyes are still bright with feverish greed.

His wife gets up and joins him at the table. She now has an enticing look on her face. She did not see what the purse contained, but she did catch its reflection in her husband's eyes. Mrs. Graubois turns to the stranger. "Well, in this town you should have no trouble in finding . . ." "I am a blacksmith," he replies, cutting her short. "In that case," the innkeeper says, "you're out of luck. There's no need for a blacksmith around here . . . We already have one, and he sure has no desire to leave the village." A brief smile flies over the stranger's mouth, but caught up in their chatter, the Graubois do not notice it. "If you were to set up shop against him, you would only get half of what you could make," adds Mrs. Graubois. "Here, there's just enough work for one." "Yes," her husband continues, "if you were a bricklayer or a carpenter, you could easily find work around here. They're always building something."

The newcomer remains silent for a moment. He then calmly repeats, "I am a blacksmith, and nothing else." "It's a pity," replies the innkeeper, as if he wanted to comfort him. For a brief moment the man seems to turn into granite as he declares, "I will be a blacksmith in Sologne, and I will forge wherever I please." Mrs. Graubois nods her head. "You'll have a long way to walk," she adds. "The Sologne is filled with blacksmiths, and everywhere sons are lying in wait for their fathers' retirements." "I have walked enough," retorts the stranger. "I will stay here."

The Graubois decide that with such a stubborn man they had better talk about something else. Right now they go out of their way to squeeze out of him a little more gold. "You will eat something, won't you?" she asks slyly. "And why not rent one of our rooms for the night?" The stranger looks at the sausage and the sauerkraut placed on the innkeepers' table. He breathes in their rich scents, and sensing them teasing his stomach, he starts eating the rest of his bread. "I guess I will," he answers between his teeth.

As she comes to wait on his table, Mrs. Graubois wants to try again to read in his eyes who he really is. She has quite a reputation in the village, since no one has ever been able to evade her scrutinizing glance. She's had that gift since birth, and she terrorizes the villagers with it. Therefore she starts to study the stranger, while he indifferently allows her to look him over. Pretending to prepare his dinner, she slowly stirs the sauerkraut as if to better spread its smell, while she ventures into his eyes. She immediately backs off: the man's glance is as steady and strong as two steel beads. All that she can briefly read in them is a warning that she had better not insist, as if talons would suddenly leap from these eyes and make sure she would never be able to use her gift again. Frightened and disoriented, she drops her fork. It hits the side of his plate and chips away a piece of porcelain. She would like to apologize, but the words strangle in her throat. Sheepishly, she goes back to her table and sits down in front of her husband.

The Graubois are now quite worried, as if this man were the visible member of a crowd of strangers silently invading the dining room. Suddenly they are startled by a raucous clamor coming from outside their house, as though a cart-load of animals had just overturned against the door. This illusion is short-lived, for the door flies open and a crowd of dismayed faces comes sprawling into the room. Sentil, the plowman, is among them, along with Vairon, the carpenter; Gomart, the miller; Laurent; Monge; and many others. All are gesticulating and shouting at the same time.

"But . . . what . . . what's happening?" squeals Mrs. Graubois, as if the stranger had just jumped on her. The men retreat to the threshold of the inn. "You haven't heard?" asks Vairon. "Christophe is dead!" add the others, whose voices are like the links of a heavy, clanging chain that they've been dragging throughout the village. "He hanged himself," whispers Gomart. Vairon has already left. It's not every day that he can run around, hawking such news. By now he must have reached the house of Courli, the baker. He must have opened the door and thrown in his "You haven't heard?" Now, sharing the same desire to spread the news to every house in the village, the men turn around and leave. Despite her astonishment, Mrs. Graubois has managed to grab the arm of one of the men as he is hurrying out. She takes him aside and questions him, while hiding from the stranger's eyes. "Gomart, could it be that someone hanged him?" she whispers.

"Who could have hanged our blacksmith?" answers the miller. "Can you imagine anyone strong enough to do that?" Mrs. Graubois turns to the stranger. She sizes up the build, the strength, and the enigmatic composure of her customer, as so many suspicions directed toward him. It suddenly dawns on her that from the moment the door opened, the man has not displayed even a hint of surprise. Mrs. Graubois is on the verge of making a few insinuations about him when Gomart escapes her and runs out to join the others.

She closes the door and looks at the stranger, who continues to eat heartily, oblivious of anything else. "Maybe you don't know who Christophe was?" she asks angrily.

"I don't have the faintest idea," the man replies impassively.

The innkeeper interrupts his wife and tries to contain his indignation as he sharply addresses the stranger. "Maybe you'll pay a bit more attention when I tell you that Christophe was our blacksmith and that he had no children or apprentice to succeed him?" The newcomer slowly wipes his plate clean with a piece of bread. When at last he condescends to look at the Graubois, they do not read in his face the interest they expect to find.

"I see," he answers in a neutral tone of voice, as he gets up from his chair.

Mrs. Graubois tries again to elicit a reaction from him. "You're a lucky man," she says cautiously.

"Maybe," replies the stranger, as he yawns and looks at the stairwell leading to the rooms. The innkeepers are so eager to see him leave that they quickly bring him a lamp, which he takes without thanking them.

"You'll find your room on the second floor; it's right in front of you as you reach the landing," says Mrs. Graubois, who does not dare look at him. He walks across the room and starts up the stairs. Each step creaks under his wooden clogs.

"By the way, what's your name?" the innkeeper calls out, now encouraged by the distance.

The stranger stops and hesitates for a moment, as if his mind were trying to return from very far away. "My name is . . . Roc," he finally answers.

"Roc who?" questions Mrs. Graubois, suddenly emboldened by her curiosity.

"Just call me Roc," retorts the stranger as he reaches the second floor and slams the bedroom door behind him. They hear the wooden floor creak and the bed moan under his body. In a second the stranger has fallen asleep without taking off his clothes. Alone in the dining room, the Graubois now feel the weight of his presence hanging heavily upon their house.

Sabeur, the old park ranger, now looks pale and distraught. He pauses before entering Christophe's forge. All the men who followed him up there, talking and shouting at one another, suddenly become silent. Their voices fade away, stifled by the presence of death. Christophe has been hanging for over an hour, but no one has dared to take him down, so the villagers have gone to Sabeur's house and convinced him that cutting the rope is part of his responsibilities. After all, the park ranger is the only one for miles around empowered with a semblance of authority.

Sabeur finally comes in. The others follow with their lamps. Craning their necks through the frame of the door, they all look like a cluster of faded sunflowers. The lights from their lamps now bathe Christophe's body in a shimmering halo. His big hands are open, his fingers stretched out like threatening claws, as if they were waiting for the first one who would dare approach them. The forge feels like a mortuary chamber. Finally, in this harrowing atmosphere, Sabeur goes to the anvil. He tries his best not to think about the dead man, but it is useless: the stiff feet of Christophe are hanging right before his eyes! Behind him, chiseled against the darkness, the villagers' faces are now completely still, as if they had turned to wood. The blacksmith's body is hanging much too high for Sabeur to reach it, and pulling on Christophe's feet will not break the rope. So he motions to one of the villagers to come and help him: pointing his finger at the rope, Sabeur shows him the exact place where it should be cut. Then it will only be a matter of easing the body down until Sabeur catches it. The man climbs on top of the anvil, and despite his queasiness he is forced to hold on to Christophe's clothes to keep his balance. He clings to the dead man while he opens his knife. All eyes are now fixed upon him and in everybody's mind dances the same inconceivable but tenacious fear that the cadaver might break off at the neck, only to leave his head caught up in the slipknot.

"Cut the rope!" shouts Sabeur, who braces himself under the body, gritting his teeth as if he expected to receive the whole ceiling on his back.

The rope is cut and the body falls, immediately caught by the man who has just set it free. He holds it for a moment; then slowly brings it down on Sabeur's back, who staggers under the weight. Everybody rushes to help, and they all feel as if they are lifting a huge sack of oats in which some prankster has hidden a few oak-tree branches. They carefully lay Christophe on the floor. Even lying down, the tall blacksmith seems to tower over them. Few men dare look at his face—a frightful image is too quickly absorbed and retained by the mind, only to become later the tool of torturous nightmares. Sabeur's hands are struggling with the knots. The first one has slipped along the rope and is stuck under the others, right up against Christophe's Adam's apple. The old ranger tries in vain to roll back the thick cartilage that, only a few hours ago, was still the blacksmith's voice. The knot stubbornly tightens, relentlessly strangling Christophe, even beyond his death.

Sabeur takes every precaution to keep his fingers out of reach of the cadaver's mouth, which remains open. The bites of the dead are sometimes poisonous. For everyone knows that as soon as the departed have passed beyond the gate of this life, they always change sides and start hating the living. (It might sound like an old wives' tale, but there must be some truth in it. After all, one wonders why we always dig each grave six feet deep, before packing down a ton of earth upon the coffin and encasing it under a heavy concrete slab . . . it's just a precaution whose meaning has now been lost.) The old park ranger is still struggling against the knots and becomes bolder. His nails scratch the skin as he slips his fingers between the rope and the neck. Christophe's head motions as if to say no. His lackluster eyes are now sprinkled with the fine reddish dust that covers the forge's floor like a

ceremonial carpeting. From a distance it looks as if the two
men have had a fierce struggle and that the outcome of the
fight is totally unexpected, for Sabeur, the winner, is old and
scrawny, while his defeated opponent is half his age and
three times his weight. The knots finally come undone. Sabeur takes the rope and buries it in his pocket, while his eyes
silently speak to the men around him, as if to say, "Later, later
. . . I'll give a piece of it to those who want a good-luck
charm."

Suddenly, between the kitchen and the forge, the blacksmith's wife appears on the threshold. She asks that her husband be carried out to the bedroom, but her voice is much
too loud and steady to be a widow's lament. Startled, the men
turn around to look at her, as if she had nothing to do with
the man who is lying on the dusty floor. Nobody has ever
liked her very much, and she has always despised the villagers. She has never sowed any love and never gathered
much kindness. No one in the room feels like comforting
her. She shows no pain at all; she's only annoyed to find so
many people where her husband used to work alone.

Four men grab hold of Christophe, and the strongest
man in the village now looks like a rolled-up piece of tar-
paulin. The blacksmith's wife precedes the procession into
the bedroom. She's only worried about the untidiness that
this whole affair brings into her house. As they walk over the
threshold, one of the bearers stumbles against the steps. A
convulsive jolt seems to run through the blacksmith's body, as
if he were brought back home by force, dead drunk and retch-
ing. In the room his widow quickly removes an expensive
bedspread made of green silk. "Wait a minute!" she orders,
as though the men were delivering some sort of carnival
dummy. "Would you wait just a minute?" She carefully folds
the bedspread and places it on a chair. She walks to Christophe and rapidly dusts his back with her hands. She fears
that all that rust might very well ruin her white sheets, but
she does not dare remove them in front of the villagers.
"Now then, go ahead!" she commands the men, while wiping
her hands on her blue apron. When the blacksmith is finally

resting on the bed, everyone passes in front of his spouse and briefly touches her hand, for tradition's sake. They do it only in memory and respect of Christophe, for in their hearts they feel more sorrow for him than for his insensitive widow.

Once they have all left, two old neighbors come in to lay out the corpse. They dress him up in his Sunday clothes. Their voices are so sad that they sound as if they were praying, while they are only gossiping between their teeth, upbraiding Christophe's wife for hesitating to use new candles at the top of the bed.

"We ought to shave him now," squawks one of the neighbors. "If we wait until tomorrow his skin will come off with his hair." At first the widow hesitates, but she takes one look at Christophe and sternly replies, "No, don't. He never wanted me to shave him anyway!"

That night, throughout the village of Brandes, everyone lies oppressed with the memory of Christophe. In their minds the same picture constantly returns. Whether it is so blurry an image that they can hardly believe it, or so real a figure that it could almost be spoken to, they all struggle against the frightful and awe-inspiring face of their strangled blacksmith. Those who did not see his mask of death imagine it as even more horrendous, an evocation that slowly turns into a morbid vision they cannot repel from their sleep.

The waves of the night finally spill forth a whitish foam, which rolls through the light gauze of the morning fog. The dawn awakens, and its bluish darkness is pierced by the rays of a widening and silent pallor, as if daybreak had to labor against its lingering shadows.

The people of Brandes have always risen with the echoes of one another's chores. This morning, they feel for the first time how much the forge had become a part of their lives, how much it was necessary to the ordered cadence of the day. As the village awakes, everyone senses the intense silence of the anvil's tune. The even rhythm of the villagers' work is now out of time. Dirier's saw is off the beat with

Vairon's hammering. The well chain grates on its own, and even the creaking of the carts sounds erratic and odd. It is as if Christophe had been some sort of noise conductor, orchestrating the village's music, forcing everyone to follow the rhythm of his hammer. But Christophe will no longer beat time. He is now lying down, cold from head to toe, wearing around his neck the purple mark where the rope has scraped off his skin. Putting the finishing touch to the blacksmith's coffin, Vairon sends throughout the village the mournful song of dry oak wood. It is a tune made of hollow notes, as hollow as the grave where Christophe will be laid today, offered to the voracious earth, whose appetite has already been whetted by Denys's digging. With each angry blow of his hammer, with each nail driven through the knotted boards, Vairon repeats the song. Though he does not realize it, his hammering pays a last tribute to Christophe, as if he tolled the bell for him, in the name of every noise and clatter of the village.

Before entering Christophe's house, Roc has to bend down under a doorway that is both too low and too wide. It is a passage made for the barrel-shaped ordinary mortals who inhabit this village, not for a tall and robust fellow like Roc. He walks into the forge and straightens up. Two women are seated in front of him: Catherine, who is Christophe's widow, and Benette, the carpenter's wife. Both are slumped in their chairs, brooding on their boredom. Pulling back the tails of his long cape over his shoulders, the stranger walks straight to the widow—oddly enough, he has never met her and yet he identifies her at once.

"Well now, here you are, all alone with this useless forge," says Roc. The moment of surprise over, Catherine stands up, and with the composure of being the proud owner of the place, she walks closer to him.

"Yes, I am," she replies, slightly distrustful, "but who are you? I've never seen you around these parts." Roc tries to smile, but all the woman can see is an eerie, menacing grin. She retreats towards her chair, while her friend hurries out of the forge and returns to the bedroom where Christophe is lying. Staring at Catherine, Roc sizes her up at a glance. He lingers on her face, on her wrinkles, and knows her age at once, as one would read into the grooves of a sawed-off tree. Catherine's head barely reaches his elbows. Not wishing to have to bend over her, Roc takes a few steps back, in order to have her full stature focused in his eyes.

"I am a blacksmith," he says harshly, in a tone that is more suitable to the kind of character he has just read in her. His voice is too loud to be appropriate in a dead man's house; his eyes are like two reddish brands embedded in his face. By the tone of his voice and the look in his eyes, he forces a blush of embarrassment to appear on the discolored cheeks of the widow, who is now totally subjugated by the stranger. "I guess that now you're not going to use the hearth and the hammer on your own," continues Roc, with the same icy grin on his lips.

Catherine briefly looks at the other woman, who has just returned to the forge, driven by an insatiable curiosity. "Of course not," she replies nervously, as if to enlist her support. Vairon's wife tries to encourage her. She emits a shrill laugh, which splutters in the forge like a long string of empty sea-shells. Irritated, Roc turns around and flings a volley of sharp words at her.

"Woman, if you have anything to do with the property of the dead man, come over here and participate; if not, you'd better get your laughter out of here before it strangles you for good." The stranger's warning rings out like a curse called upon her. Vairon's wife turns pale and dashes out of the forge.

Now that they are alone, Roc looks at Catherine while putting his hands in his pockets.

"You have to find a successor for the forge," he tells her, while his fingers start to jingle a few coins. Christophe's widow immediately recognizes the unmistakable song of gold coins.

"Of course," she replies in a feverish voice. "Of course I want to sell. Have you ever seen a blacksmith's widow trying to succeed her husband?" The stranger nods in agreement, while a shower of golden sparks bursts from his eyes, spurring on Catherine's cupidity.

"I have with me enough gold to take all your worries away; I'll make you a good deal," continues Roc. But before proceeding any further, he takes pleasure in fueling the widow's greed with the pangs of an interminable silence. Finally, when he resumes the tickling sound of jingled coins, he starts questioning her. "You must have thought about selling this forge more than once," sneers Roc, "like tonight for instance, and maybe the night before . . . I'd bet you've been thinking about it for years."

"Well, I . . . I . . ." stutters Catherine, as her most secret wish has been so easily uncovered. She now realizes that in spite of the stranger's apparent generosity, she will have to abide by his will. "How much . . . how much do you think all this is worth?" asks the widow, while her arm spans the forge as if to enhance the value of "all this." With bountiful and waving gestures she unscrupulously cuts and divides Christophe's property. But as her hand reaches the half-open door of the bedroom, where the blacksmith's body is resting, she pauses before quickly closing the door. For a moment her face has taken on a look of terror, as if she feared that her husband would suddenly get up and shout his indignation with a terrifying and threatening scream, as only the dead are capable of when they are infuriated.

Roc smiles while the coins continue to tinkle under his tantalizing fingers. "He must have a hundred of them," thinks Catherine, quickly brought back to reality by the sound of gold. "What's your price?" she asks, panting. "We can settle this fast. You'll get the house and the forge, and I'll go live with my sister at Aubigny. I'll let you have everything!" Roc slowly takes his hand out of his pocket, and the hand that has been toying with the widow's tormented avidity is now full of shining gold coins. To make sure she is not dreaming, Catherine immediately asks if she can touch them. Roc stretches out his hand, and she grabs a coin, feverishly inspecting it. She looks at the date and sees that it has been recently stamped out. The coin is so warm that it feels as if it could have been minted a few hours ago. The widow snatches the gold and starts counting with trembling fingers, each time begging for more with an imploring look in her eyes.

When his hand has been emptied for the fifth time, Roc leaves it open under the widow's stare, in order to make her understand that she has reached the number of coins he is willing to pay. Catherine clasps the gold in her apron, as if she had just captured an exotic bird. The grin that had been the only sign of life on the stranger's face has now vanished, and as he addresses the widow, his words come out like pieces of broken glass.

"As soon as your man is in the ground, I don't want to see you around here."

"He'll be buried today," she answers quickly, as if she had never even thought of burying him at all. "He'll be in his grave this afternoon, and I'll be gone tonight!"

"Fine," replies Roc. "Now I'll take a closer look at this forge you sold me for twice its price." And as the widow obsequiously hastens to show him around, he snarls, "I don't need anyone, leave this house, now!"

Alone in the room Roc slowly inhales the scents of metal and rust, and for a long time he remains there, sensually breathing in the fragrance of the forge. In the corner the anvil seems to float over the scrap iron and the dust that cover the floor. On the workbench the tools are standing up, their wooden handles smoothed out and softened by the harsh chafing of Christophe's calloused hands. They look like old yellowed candles, left in disarray on an abandoned altar.

The stranger's feet find what his eyes cannot see. At the noise they make when he steps on them, he quickly makes an inventory of the other tools. There are the tongs, and over there the pliers, the clamps, and the pincers. Continuing his inspection, Roc does not even look at the piece of rope that remains hanging from a beam, the one Christophe chose as his passageway between life and death. Removing his cape, the stranger takes hold of one of the sledgehammers. His hands tighten around the cold handle as he feels the weight of the tool. He strikes the anvil twice, and a clear sound rings out in the forge. With this fist of metal he could flatten an iron bar in less than forty blows. With even more power he strikes a third time, just to show the steel who is its new master. He pounds the anvil with so much force that it gives out a clang, which almost sounds like a cry of pain.

"Please!" Suddenly, behind him, a frightened and tiny voice has just materialized in the dark. The stranger had thought he was alone, of that he was certain, for no one has ever managed to startle him like this. He has been followed without his knowing it, but how could anyone have succeeded in deceiving him? . . . He who knows everything! He turns around but he sees nothing. He can only hear a soft and rapid breathing in the obscurity. Gradually, near the black hood that covers the cold hearth, he discerns a lightsome figure slowly coming toward him.

It's a girl. Her awkwardness and her fragile adolescent body covered with a straw-colored sweater make her look like a doll. The pale and intermittent light that reaches into the forge cannot tarnish the radiating fairness of her long hair. Even though she appears to be about sixteen years old, her face is still that of a child. Now that she is close to him, Roc unleashes from his eyes the piercing gaze that subjugates anyone who dares approach him. But what he reads in her mind is not fear; it is instead the peacefulness of a quiet lake. For the first time Roc is disconcerted. He sees in her eyes an endless bluish path. Intrigued, he follows it and lets himself be lured further. He keeps going and soon reaches into an aquamarine labyrinth, when suddenly he realizes that the implacable power of his mind will shatter itself if he takes another step forward. Closing his eyes, he struggles to avert her glance, for he now fears that she might see what is within him and beyond . . . that she might find out *who* he really is!

Roc shifts his attention to the girl's features. They are gracefully unaffected and regular, giving her a look of undefiled seductiveness. The charm of this face slowly draws him back to her eyes, into boundless pupils, which continue to beguile and unsettle him. The stranger tries a different approach.

"What are you doing here?" he bawls out, spitting out each syllable as if he wanted to shatter the mirror of her eyes, the wall against which his own piercing gaze is being edged off. The girl's lips do not move, but suddenly her eyes widen, trying to say something by changing their color, as if she could modulate the tone of each word that her mouth cannot speak. She then turns around and walks back to kneel down near the dormant hearth. Resting her chin on the ledge, she remains motionless before the cold ashes of the abandoned coals. Roc understands that she has resumed a long and patient wait to which she seems to be accustomed. He comes to her and puts his hand on her naked shoulder. Her bones are fragile but her skin is soft and warm. As he touches her, Roc feels a brief shiver under his palm, the shiver of a wild animal startled by a man's first stroke. She does not turn around to look at him, for her eyes are fixed upon the black coldness of the forge. Roc reads in her mind and discovers the nature of her yearning. He goes to the grate, and throwing a fistful of dry twigs upon it, he lights them with disconcerting ease. The thought of fire and smoke has barely materialized in his mind before the hearth is engulfed with flames, while the coals instantly redden and begin to crackle. With its first breaths, the fire assails the darkness and routs it out of the forge. The girl lifts up her head, and pressing her long and delicate fingers upon her mouth, she moans with delight. Roc hears her and starts pulling on the chain that forces the air out of the bellows. A flight of sparkles passes over the girl's eyes. They are now as stirred up as the coals, and as Roc channels a whirlwind into the ravenous fire, he subdues them both at the same time.

Still troubled by his inability to unsettle her, the stranger decides to make the flames roar even louder. Leaving the bellows, he comes to the fire and starts blowing his own breath on the coals. The flames surge and soar higher and higher, while the bricks of the hearth start cracking, as if they were retreating from this unearthly blaze. But the girl is not frightened; she simply turns around and whispers, "Thank you, Christophe," as calmly as if she were addressing the dead blacksmith.

Roc's laughter bursts forth and almost drowns the roaring flames. To think he was afraid of this child! She cannot even recognize anyone!

"I am not Christophe," he tells her gently. "My name is Roc."

"Roc," she repeats, not the least bit surprised as the stranger sits down beside her. "But . . . Christophe . . . make fire?" asks the girl.

"Roc makes fire too, even better!" answers the stranger, who smiles openly for the first time. And then, still transfixed by the flames, she asks, "Where . . . Christophe?" But before he can answer, the door of the forge opens, revealing Catherine cautiously peering into the room while she remains on the threshold. She fears the stranger, but when she heard the sound of the bellows, she had to come and take a look. As if to exorcise the memory of Christophe from her mind, she needs to see the forge run by someone else, so that it becomes the last remembrance of her life in this village.

But as soon as she sees the girl, Catherine hurries across the room and grabs her by the arm. Roc stands up as she unleashes her spitefulness against the young maid. He recognizes the same malevolence that he subdued an hour ago with a handful of gold. He walks to the widow, and the look in his eyes makes her retreat so hastily that she almost falls back on the steps.

"But don't . . . don't you know who she is?" whines Catherine, scared and stupefied at his reaction. "I just wanted to be of service by ridding you of this little vermin!"

"I don't suppose she is your daughter?" asks the stranger.

"Good Lord, no!" protests Catherine, who looks up to the sky. "May God shield me from such a catastrophe!" Roc flinches, as if a sudden twinge had just shot through his body.

"Shut up, woman," he thunders. "Go pray somewhere else than here!"

"But you don't understand," retorts the widow vehemently, as if to warn him. "It's Isabelle . . . she's the village idiot! Can't you see that she's retarded? She's crazy as a loon. I'm telling you, you've got to be careful with those people . . . run her out of here!" Catherine turns to the young girl. "You're going to leave right now!" she yells. "I told you a hundred times to go back wherever you came from—we don't want you around here!"

Isabelle remains cloaked in her gentle indifference. Now that the fire no longer brightens up her eyes, she has retreated into her own world.

"You see, you see," continues the widow, "there's nothing but a void in her eyes . . . One day she's going to hurt somebody . . . I used to warn my husband about her, but he would never listen to me! Who knows if she doesn't have something to do with . . ." While the widow is chattering, Roc feels a tiny arm softly brushing against his side. Gently, he takes the young girl's hand and puts it in his. A shower of sparks instantly returns to her eyes and revives them.

"Isabelle . . . that's a pretty name," says the stranger.

"Christophe?" asks the girl suddenly, scratching his hand.

"Christophe is gone," replies Roc, as the widow points her finger to the piece of rope that hangs from the beams.

"He's gone thataway," she tells her, and neither her hand nor her voice betrays the slightest hint of regret. Isabelle looks at the rope and does not understand.

"Come back . . . same way?" she asks the widow.

"No, you don't come back after you're dead," says Catherine, laughing. "That'd be too easy!" Isabelle's eyes turn dark blue, as if she is struggling to comprehend something far beyond her understanding, but she gives up. Her eyes close and tears start running down her cheeks. Imperturbed, the widow casually looks at the piece of rope, and without another word she turns around and leaves the forge.

Two months have passed since Christophe's burial, when one muggy Sunday morning a rattling tilbury rushes past the first houses of the village. Drawn by a mettlesome horse, it finally screeches to a halt over the coarse cobblestones of the marketplace. Dressed in an astrakhan coat, a middle-aged man steps off. He removes his delicate leather gloves and demands in a condescending tone to be shown the way to the forge. Satisfied, he jumps back into the tilbury and whips his horse so harshly that the fiery animal bucks and nearly breaks off the shafts. Driving around the church, the carriage cuts straight through the linden trees before stopping in front of the blacksmith's house. The man quickly throws his whip onto the seat and hastens to open the side door of the coach. He cautiously takes a bundle of white linen, which a fur-clad woman hands him. Then, oblivious of the mud puddles that soil their clothes, the couple crosses the courtyard and knocks on Roc's door.

The villagers follow them at a distance. They all know that for centuries every blacksmith of the village of Brandes has been endowed with mysterious healing powers. No one really knows when it all began or where those secrets originated, not even the local priests, who had vainly sought to put an end to them. It was only understood by all that these gifts emanated from the ground on which the forge stood and that they seemed to be automatically bestowed upon each new blacksmith, whether he wanted them or not. No one could recall that Christophe had ever used them. He would not even talk about them, for he was convinced that these powers were unholy.

Such was not the case with Roc. The ancestral tradition had been well perpetuated in him. It did not take a month before his reputation spread beyond the village, especially his power to heal the diseases that would usually cut down many young children during the harsh winter months. But if Roc had already welcomed dozens of desperate parents who were now praising his talents to the incredulous ears and mocking glances of their physicians, he had also attracted against himself the concerted hostility of the entire village. For a reason known only to him, the blacksmith had steadfastly refused to cure any of his neighbors' ills. No one had managed to make him change his mind, not even Mrs. Graubois, who had spent hours vainly crying and banging on

the blacksmith's door, while her husband remained chained
to the village square fountain, panting and rolling on the
ground, agonizing in the throes of rabies. Even though his
savage shouts were loud enough to churn everybody's stomach, the door of the forge had remained resolutely shut.

Crazed with grief, Mrs. Graubois had finally run home,
only to return to the village square and cut short her husband's torments with one blast of his shotgun. No one had
ever notified the authorities. Even Sabeur had turned a blind
eye to the discreet burial that followed. But if the cold earth
had finally muzzled the innkeeper's bestial screams, a vengeful and silent hatred now inhabited all the villagers, as they
cursed both their blacksmith and the cures he dispensed only
to unknown children from other counties. And so today's
tilbury was just bringing another sick baby from another sick
town, where people dressed extravagantly and snubbed the
countryside and its common folk, even on the day when the
lives of their children might suddenly depend upon the talents of a rural blacksmith.

Yet somehow, for no apparent reason, today's arrival
seems different. Something awakens the villagers from their
vindictive passivity, as though the fear that the blacksmith
has woven into their minds were unexpectedly stifled by a
new and pressing curiosity. A few men get up from their
benches and boldly cross the courtyard. Through the tiny
cracks of the building, they can now see the inside of the
forge. So they stand, their eyes riveted to the wall, peering
for the first time into Roc's mysterious abode. They are unaware that the scene they are about to witness will reveal a
great deal about the new blacksmith—indeed, far more than
they had ever wanted to know.

Seeing the couple coming in, Roc shows no surprise at
all, as if he had been expecting them. He closes the door and
goes to the bellows to stir up the flames of the hearth. For a
while he moves about the forge as if he were alone. Disconcerted, the man in the astrakhan coat realizes he will have
to speak condescendingly, in order to impress upon Roc the
superior stature of his social rank. Strangely enough, his

friends in the city had depicted the healer as a simple rural blacksmith, when in fact he is now facing a country squire.

"Sir," starts the man with a feigned politeness that exasperates Roc, "Sir, our son suffers from convulsions . . . We have tried everything . . . The physicians cannot help us . . . but we've been told that you . . . you could cure him. You are our last hope . . . I am a wealthy man . . ." His wife is standing behind him, nervously nibbling at her cambric handkerchief. She rushes to the blacksmith and puts her delicate hand on his powerful and sweaty arm.

"I beg of you . . . save him . . . We'll pay you whatever you want!"

Roc pushes her back toward her husband. He removes his huge leather apron and wipes the top of the anvil with it, dusting off the pieces of gray skin that form the bark of untamed iron. He then turns to the father.

"I don't want any money; the only payment I require is to become the godfather of this child," he says quietly. "That is, if I can cure him, of course," he adds after a moment of silence, as if trifling with the parents' despair. They do not understand what he could stand to gain by such an agreement, but the father silently makes up his mind. "First of all, my son's cure . . . later on, we'll have enough money to dissuade him from this eccentric demand. I must do nothing to upset this fellow . . ."

"Of course," he replies quickly, while handing the child over to the blacksmith, "and since we all agree, let us not waste any more time." But Roc has read his thoughts. He takes a piece of paper out of his pocket and almost flings it into his face.

"You sign here," commands the blacksmith. Taken by surprise with this unexpected artifice, which prevents him from going back on his word, the man glances helplessly at his wife while he clutches an old and ornate fountain pen. He signs the document, and Roc finally takes the screaming baby in his arms, as if somehow the two men had just clinched a deal.

The linen that covered the baby is quickly removed as

Roc lays him down naked on the anvil. The cold of the steel instantly penetrates his back and suffocates him. Despite the infant's shrill cries of protest, all eyes are now fixed upon the blacksmith as he undergoes a strange metamorphosis. His face changes into an alien glower. His features harden while his eyes take on the menacing stare of a hawk. Terrorized, the child remains transfixed by this ghastly mask, which fascinates him and strangles his tears. The young mother rushes to the anvil to retrieve her son, but the blacksmith turns around, and when their eyes meet she stops as if she had collided with a glass wall.

"Hold your son down by his shoulders," snarls Roc at the father. The infant struggles both against the chilling cold of the anvil and the sweltering heat of the hearth. But deep inside him, the pains are slowly disappearing. Soon he can only feel the scratching of his father's trembling fingernails. His sobbing has stopped and an unknown peace now flows through his senses. At the very moment the child has reached an almost serene quietness, Roc starts to roar like a feline leaping onto a patiently awaited prey. In a single move he tears off his shirt, and the ripping of the cloth reveals the brutish might of his bronzelike chest. His hands grab his heaviest sledgehammer. He raises it so high that for an instant he stands on his toes before bringing it down on the baby, howling so forcefully that he freezes the heart of every onlooker.

Instinctively the father has almost drawn back his son, whose body shrivels up like a threatened porcupine, but he manages to collect himself just long enough to allow this enactment to take place. He knows that it is only a part of a ritual that has been carefully described to him before he came to the village. But at the sight of her son about to be crushed to death, the mother faints and collapses face down on the rust-covered floor. The steel mass is about to smash the baby's head when Roc suddenly stops the course of the sledgehammer with an abrupt constriction of his muscles, ending the seemingly deadly blow in a light brushing of the tool against the skin of his young patient. The child bursts into tears, and his cries of deliverance are as many piercing blades into the flesh of the horrified villagers, hidden behind the walls. The father hurriedly dresses the baby while his wife struggles to her feet. Now that their son is cured, they only want to run away. They stagger outside, blinking at the sun, and rush to the tilbury. With one crack of the whip, the carriage rattles away in a trail of mud and rust.

His back against the wall, Roc remains still, with his eyes closed and his arms folded. Suddenly he shivers: a slow and soft caress is running up his arm, while a light breath brushes against his skin. Looking down, he sees Isabelle's face. And Roc, the man-beast, the savage executioner, feels his lassitude leaving him as his face creases into a smile. He tries to pull himself together, but he is subdued once more by that satin cheek gently stroking his chest.

"You . . . fire . . . fire and light," whispers Isabelle, while she presses her lips where the blacksmith's heart is pounding wildly.

Ensconced in the surrounding obscurity, Roc has fallen asleep on the bare floor. His body is so completely motionless that he looks like a marmorean statue. A quiet lapping has now replaced the familiar sounds of the forge, but its faint echo gradually breaks the silence and reaches into the black-smith's consciousness. He remains still as he awakes, and barely parting his eyelids, his piercing gaze cuts through the darkness. Facing the dormant redness of the hearth, Isabelle is kneeling down before a huge water pail adorned with a stiff cluster of pincers and tongs. Drawing the grayish water in the hollow of her hand, she bathes her face. Pretending to be sound asleep, Roc closely watches the girl, and as he pores over her an unfamiliar and vibrant emotion starts to arouse him.

Isabelle slowly continues to wet her face, which reflects the reddish-brown shadows of the embers, as though she were trying to cool down the oppressive heat of an unknown fever. Her silky tresses stick to the mist of her cheeks. She patiently gathers her hair and twists it into a bun with a strand of hemp that she finds lying on the floor. Roc can see her long neck upon which her hand lets the water trickle down. He holds his breath, as if he fears that it could shatter this moment, this image pressing against the unyielding power of his will. Unaware of his presence, Isabelle starts to unbutton her frayed blouse and bares one of her shoulders, caressing it with her cheek. Roc looks at her naked arm. He sees a slender hand come to rest upon her other shoulder. He follows her long fingers as they leisurely return to stroke her neck. Overwhelmed by a sensual delight that she cannot control, Isabelle sighs and moans. Her mouth opens, as if she could scream the wildness of her excitement, but she can only whisper the blacksmith's name, and this ecstatic murmur becomes a throbbing quarrel that pierces Roc's impregnable heart.

How could Isabelle ever fathom the measure of silent torture that she is unwittingly inflicting upon him? Both the jailer and the captive of her unbridled sensuality, she slowly continues to remove her clothes. Chiseled against the shadowy light of the hearth, the outline of her naked body thrashes the blacksmith's senses with repeated lashing strokes.

Roc knows he should have closed his eyes a long time ago, but by his own device he is also subordinated to his human disguise. His veil is that of a sturdy and vigorous man, a body in which every fiber is gradually drawn toward the girl. He is now so tempted to have a taste of human passion and lust that a sough of desire escapes from his mouth. Startled, Isabelle turns around, and through the slit of his eyelids she immediately sees the phosphorescent fleck of his pupils. Her only defense is to cover her breasts with her hands. Roc remains as motionless as a bird of prey ready to swoop down upon its victim. Isabelle falls full-length on the floor, as if she could hide her head in the dust, but she is already ensnared by the frightening object of her desire as she starts to crawl toward the blacksmith. She looks up at him. The dust of the forge has daubed her face with a mask of iron scales, and this sight arouses Roc even more, as his mind starts to reel under the intensity of his first carnal hunger. Isabelle's hair comes undone and spreads upon her naked shoulders. She stands up, revealing her dust-covered breasts, firm and provocative . . . Now that she is close to the blacksmith, her tears give way to a passionate yearning. She is still frightened, but her fear is also interlaced with an irresistible attraction. When her hand finally touches his face, Roc smiles as he closes his eyes. Her quivering and lithe body falls into his arms, which immediately girth the young animal who has come to be consumed in his desire.

Now that he has succumbed to man's most powerful instinct, Roc struggles to pull himself together. He knows that his invulnerability has been violated for a brief moment, as if he had been stripped of his powers. He jumps to his feet and quickly walks to the hearth. Violently awakening the embers, he throws a handful of scrap iron upon them. When the tongs remove the reddish, contorted mass, he hurls it onto the anvil and starts to flatten it with lightning blows, as if his sledgehammer could forge a seal over the wedge that the girl has driven into him.

The clamor of Roc's anger abruptly brings Isabelle back to the reality of the forge. Within her, embers and pains, strength and gentleness are slowly abating. The shock of the blacksmith's embrace has been so great that her quiet madness starts to falter. Soon she stands amidst the infinite ramifications of a thousand things that unveil themselves before her eyes for the very first time, streaking her dormant intellect with knowledge, awakening her mind. First, she notices the flames of the hearth. Before Roc possessed her they were nothing but a cluster of warm colors, but now she sees the eeriness of their raging beauty. She finds herself at the center of this immense forge she had always found so empty. Today the room is populated by a crowd of objects and tools, all coming alive amidst the wild dancing of impish shadows. In the instant that Isabelle asks herself the reason for such a strange metamorphosis, a flood of words surges into her head: thousands of words now readily familiar to her, even though she has never learned a single one of them. Her

mind discovers how she could weave them into endless sentences . . .how she could describe what she now understands
. . . how she could tell Roc the way she feels . . .

Her eyes caress the figure of the blacksmith, and where
others see only brute force and cruel features she discerns
strength and weakness, power and tenderness. She stands up
and wants to run to him, but she falls in the dust, overwhelmed with joy and delight. As the blacksmith gently lifts
her up in his arms she whispers, "Thank you, Roc . . . Thank
you!" Standing alone with her in the forge, Roc discovers
that he has drawn her out of her chaos, that *he*, of all people,
has given her back her mind a thousandfold, as if a spark of
righteousness had escaped him, through the flaw that Isabelle had found in his armor of fire and ice. For the first time
ever he bows his head, as he feels rushing within him the dis-
cordant streams of his greatest joy poisoned by the wrath of
envenomed bitterness.

Denys is the first one to witness Isabelle's transformation. That afternoon, when he sees her leaning over the cop-
ing of the well, he fears that she might fall in. Rushing toward the girl, he seizes her around the waist and brings her
back to the ground. She was drawing a bucket of water for
the forge. As Denys gets it for her, he feels compelled to lecture the young girl with the kind of language everyone uses
with her: very short sentences made of simple words, a sort
of patter perfectly suited for toddlers and animals. But as he
looks at her, Denys suddenly stops his gesticulating speech.
He cannot continue because Isabelle's eyes, stripped of their
usual emptiness, are as alive as his. He stands there for a
minute, gaping in amazement at the laughing and mischie-
vous look of what used to be the dull stare of the village idiot.
Her eyes no longer reflect the dizziness that used to force the
villagers to look away while talking to her. Her blue eyes are
now steady and expressive, and when she speaks to him, it is
with a clear and unlabored voice, with words that sound light
and transparent.

"Thank you, Denys, thank you. But I could have drawn

the water myself. I am quite used to it by now," she says, punctuating each word with a charming and beautiful smile. Denys lets her walk back toward the forge. He remains standing by the well, as astounded as if one of the statues of the nearby church had suddenly decided to climb down from its niche, just to warm up its stiff legs.

Soon it is the turn of Courli, the baker, to be dumbfounded. After distinctly hearing Isabelle ordering a loaf of bread, he watches her in disbelief as she carefully counts the change that his wife hands back to her. She is so mystified that she does not even dare to short-change the girl, as she has always done in the past.

The news quickly spreads among the villagers, but when everyone has heard that Isabelle has been miraculously cured, they immediately brand this extraordinary transformation as yet another malefaction from their sinister blacksmith.

Ever since she has been a widow, because of Roc's refusal to heal her husband, Mrs. Graubois harbors such hatred toward the blacksmith that nothing can restrain her whenever she has the chance to malign him. Today's event is the kind of opportunity she's been waiting for. Like a bluebottle buzzing against a windowpane, she starts to tattle from door to door. She has no difficulty finding a receptive audience because she has an uncanny ability to spell out loud what everyone thinks, but is too afraid to say. At first it looks as if she will succeed only in enlisting the begrudging support of a few villagers, but by the end of the day she has managed to assemble a swarm of hatred: thirty men, who are now following her back to the inn. Facing her audience, Mrs. Graubois climbs on top of a table.

"We don't want this wretched blacksmith among us any more!" she holds forth. "Everyone can see that he doesn't belong in this village, that he has never wanted to! Ever since he settled down here, we've had more ill winds and calamities than we would ever get in a year of Sundays. First there was my husband's death—rest his soul—then came all these sick babies, and you all know by now with what strange ritual he heals them, while your own children are dying next door to his house. And today that retarded bitch parades among us as if she had more brains than you and me put together. But has any one of you ever noticed that Roc works day and night and that we've never seen a single piece of iron coming out of his forge? I'm telling you, there's something more in this arrogant monster than just his powers to heal babies, there's something else!"

"Damn it, she's right!" whisper a few men, stirred up by her words.

"You, Vairon," she continues, lowering her voice, "and you, Denys, you'd better wake up. If he has the power to cure Isabelle's madness, he could very well do the opposite and turn all of you into a bunch of dribbling morons! Sabeur, Gomart, Courli, how would you like to be the next village idiot?" Mrs. Graubois pauses and grins. She knows that such an insinuation is bound to shake them. They all remember how cruel they had been with Didier, the retarded veteran who used to limp his way around the village like a wandering and famished old dog, and who finally died of exposure a few weeks before Isabelle came to take his place.

Feeling that she will never have another opportunity, the innkeeper's widow urges the men to run the blacksmith out of town this very day, even if they have to use force. Intoxicated by her anger, the group of villagers soon turns into an angry mob, shaking their fists in agreement. Mrs. Graubois steps off the table, and walking to the far end of the dining room, she takes down from the wall the shotgun of her late husband. "There, you take it," she tells Courli, out of breath. In front of the other men the baker dares not refuse, and he grabs the weapon as the widow slips a handful of shells into his pocket. When the villagers see the determined look on his face, they all run home to get their rifles. Half an hour later, Mrs. Graubois has become the leader of a band of armed mercenaries making their way to the forge.

As they draw nearer to the blacksmith's lair the villagers feel their angry outburst wavering, but the widow has anticipated that. She hurries to the back of the group and plants in everyone's ears the seeds of a renewed outrage. They reach the linden trees, and by now they can see the door of the outlander's shop. That was the name they had finally given to Christophe's successor, to the man who terrifies them, to this blacksmith who seems to have no past, no friends, and no family. But once again an insidious fear seems to hinder their steps. They slow down. Half the villagers take up positions behind the huge trees of the main square, while the other half retreat to the safety of the church. Even those who have hidden behind the lindens have to put on a bragging air, in order to better hide their growing apprehension and cowardice.

However, unbeknownst to the others, Gomart has drunk half a bottle of gin to give himself some courage. As if he were carrying the anger of the entire village, the miller continues to walk and arrives alone in front of the forge. Brandishing his shotgun, he starts screaming in the silence, "We all want you to leave, Roc . . . we want you to get out of our village, now!" He shouts so vehemently that the vapors of alcohol come together in his head, bursting like firecrackers. Thinking that all the others are still behind him, he takes a few more steps toward the door. The villagers are now quite worried by the sudden boldness of the miller. Mrs. Graubois stands still between Vairon and Courli, who are hidden behind a stone bench. The two men cannot bring themselves to show their fears in the presence of the widow. They suddenly understand the driving force of the miller's surprising temerity, and they are terrified at the thought of becoming the target of the blacksmith's wrath, as if it were going to ascend through the chimney of his house and swoop down on them. Had they but known the consequences of their acts, they would have stood up and run back home without the loss of another moment.

Already the door of the smithy opens, revealing Isabelle's frail silhouette. Gomart immediately takes his anger out on her.

"Get the hell out of my way, you little freak!" The young girl is not in the least intimidated, as she looks at the miller and answers him with a soft, crystalline voice.

"Why are you shouting at Roc? What has he done to you? Please tell me. If I can help you, I'll be glad to . . . Roc always listens to me." The miller is frantically pointing his shotgun in every direction, as if he wanted to shoot down the entire building. Trying to appease him, Isabelle puts her hand on his arm. "Do be careful," she continues. "It could go off accidentally and hurt somebody." Gomart is no longer in control of himself.

"That's the idea!" he screams at her. "I'm gonna kill this Roc of yours, and I'll blow your brains out if you don't step aside!" Carried away by a raging outburst of defiance, he shoves her aside with a vicious slap in the face. Before he can do anything else, the huge panes of the door suddenly fly open and Roc appears, his bare chest suffused with a fiery light. He stands there, formidable, towering over the miller, and his immobility is far more frightening than any threatening gestures he could make.

Gomart is so stupefied that his drunkenness disappears in an instant, leaving him disarmed before the man he has so recklessly provoked. The miller turns around, looking for his friends, but he cannot see them. Finding himself at the center of such a deadly void, Gomart is stricken with panic. Something in the darker corner of his soul has just made him realize that he has haphazardly set foot in hell. Dropping his gun, the miller runs away from the forge. However, two apparently ordinary objects seem to suddenly materialize in his path: an old rake full of leaves, and a few steps ahead, a piece of broken bottle resting on its bottom. In his haste, Gomart does not notice them. His feet stumble over the rake handle, and as he falls full length on the ground, the sharp glass teeth slit his throat open as if a razor blade had just been driven across his neck. Hidden near the church, everyone witnesses the miller's abrupt fall, but no one is aware that he could be hurt. Only when Gomart gets back on his feet and desperately tries to close the gaping wound with his hands do the villagers see his blood squirting through his fingers, staining his white shirt with a widening crimson ruffle. The miller staggers for a moment and then collapses like an ox felled by a hammer. A few jolts continue to wrench his body, like so many useless blows against the hastening reaper.

Roc has not moved from his place, and none of the villagers dares go and rescue Gomart, lest he should also fall victim to the other invisible traps that must surround the house. Isabelle is the only one to hurry to the miller. She leans over him, and the sight of so much blood overwhelms her. As her distress deepens into sorrow, she calls out to the blacksmith, who remains silently motionless, as if he were painted on the threshold.

"Save him! Please save him," she implores Roc, calling upon her tears to better entreat him. The villagers are now aghast and powerless as they behold the nightmarish scene. They can hear Isabelle's pleas, and despite themselves their hopes also turn to the one they had come to drive out of town. They all know he has the power to save the miller's life. Even Mrs. Graubois finds herself wishing he would do it.

As he finally moves from the door, the blacksmith turns to the young girl and utters only a single word. "Come!" His outstretched arm bespeaks such an inflexible will that Isabelle cannot resist him. She obediently walks back to the house. Roc follows her and the massive oak door slams behind them, sending an echo that reaches the church and thunders against its walls. The explosion suddenly releases the villagers from the petrification that had taken hold of them. Mrs. Graubois is the first to get a grip on herself. Vairon, Courli, Denys, and all the others soon pull themselves together. They do not waste much time in deciding their next move. Roc's blood is now the price they must exact to avenge the miller's death. Their fingers poised on the triggers of their guns, they all regroup and descend upon the forge.

Back inside the shop, Roc returns to the hearth and resumes his interrupted work, as if nothing had ever happened outside. Isabelle throws herself down on her knees and clasps one of his legs in her arms.

"Roc!" she moans. "I beseech you, save him!" The blacksmith's only answer is to brutally shake her off his leg. "Roc!" she cries plaintively as she collapses on the ground and takes her head in her hands. Her sobbing reaches deep inside the blacksmith, and he can feel his inexorable decision starting to waver. But his hands suddenly become fists as he thrashes the air around him. With a firm voice Roc repeats his irrevocable verdict.

"No! I will not save him. This man got what he deserved . . . I corrected him. Besides, it is too late; there is nothing I can do for him now." Stunned by the harshness of his tone, Isabelle stands up, and for the first time, her eyes and her heart seem to penetrate deeper into him. The young girl backs away and looks at the blacksmith with intensity.

"Roc . . . are you not a holy man?" she asks in a slow and faltering voice. The blacksmith briefly closes his eyes. He hesitates for a moment and then abruptly regains his poise.

"No, Isabelle, I am not!" he replies, gritting his teeth. The girl feels her heart wrung by despair. In her disarray, she hopes to find in herself the power to save the man agonizing in the courtyard. She rushes to the door and opens it. Roc screams and tries to grab her, but she is already outside when the echoes of a volley of shots ring out in the forge.

Blinded by the flashes of the guns, Isabelle doubles up under the pain that explodes in her stomach, while her chest is hacked by a hundred shavings of lead. A purple haze rises up before her, erasing her voice and her thoughts. Her legs buckle under a formidable weight that suddenly presses down upon her shoulders. She collapses near the baker as a piercing wind mangles her body, dragging her over the stones of the courtyard. Her mind struggles to escape the precipitous depth of a dark abyss that abruptly sunders the ground of the forge. For a moment she can see a strange mosaic made of contorted faces and uneven pieces of sky, spinning above her as she continues to fall further and further below . . . The twitching body of the young girl tenses up in a last spasm, and she is no more. The villagers recoil in horror. They had only meant to rid themselves of the black-smith, and they have just murdered a child. They had all recognized the frail silhouette of Isabelle as she was dashing out of the forge, but their rifles had fired instantly, as if their hands had been inexplicably set in motion against their will.

None of them can step back as Roc comes out of the forge, wearily dragging his long black cape, which he places upon the dead body. The villagers cannot even begin to run away when he walks up to the group. In the oppressive silence he scornfully stares at each one of them before bending down and picking up Isabelle. Then, oblivious of the cold, the outlander clutches her against his bare chest. Leaving the murderers impaled upon agonizing shivers, he allows them to see the impossible—the sight of his tears running down a face that for an instant had become human. He then turns around and starts back on the road that leads to nowhere.

The Last Rites

THAT night Pierre was even more miserable than usual. Lying awake, he fretfully awaited his wife's return, feeling once more in his heart the sadness of his frustrated love. Lucie had vanished once again to sleep in someone else's arms.

The townsfolk and the educated still think of peasants as two-legged animals. They also believe that their hearts are daubed with manure and that they probably have no more sensitivity than an ox. Born of the mind of city dwellers, this idea has ascribed to farmers emotions made of brambles and cudgels. But under the wild bark of these so-called bumpkins there quivers the delicate sap of sweet tenderness.

As if to lend some truth to this old urban prejudice, Pierre was known as a hardhearted man. Shouting every day at his farmhands, he had a well-deserved reputation of always being temperamental. Yet Pierre was honest: he was equally incapable of vileness or of simpering ways. As if he were the embodiment of the elements directing the course of the day in the countryside, Pierre could alternately become as violent as the thunder, as cold as the north wind, and as hot-blooded as the sun at high noon. Around the farm his workers were well aware of his changing disposition, but they would not have left to work anywhere else, even for better wages. If they stayed in spite of his short temper, it was because anyone in the pay of Pierre knew that he would learn what farming was all about. Pierre could teach how to en-

Originally published as "Mais qui est le plus fort?" in Claude Seignolle, *Contes sorciers*, Verviers (Belgium): Gérard, 1974
© 1974 by Claude Seignolle

courage the grain to grow high and strong; he could show you secret ways to better fatten your cattle. The helpers understood very well what Lucie could not even fathom. They all agreed that she was much too green for him, anyway. Fifteen years younger than Pierre, Lucie wasn't interested in anything save her proclivity to cuckold her husband. That was enough to create a thick hedge of discord between them, and today the only passageways that remained through this hedge were the rare moments that they would still share in bed.

Still Lucie could drive Pierre dizzy with desire. It was as if the caresses of this delicate and fragrant flower were transmuted in his senses as so many bright colors and passionate words of love. But when all was said and done, their union looked like the mating of a doe and a plowshare. They fared so poorly together that each time Lucie felt her husband wanting her desperately, she would use even the flimsiest of excuses to flee the farm and go to the rescue of an unknown bedridden great-aunt. Or she would travel fifty miles to celebrate the birthday of a cousin three times removed. Actually, Lucie was deceiving her husband with another man, much gentler than he. But Pierre was not fooled by her pretenses. Rather, he chose to wait and suffer the twinges of his languishing and impotent distress.

And so that night, his bed once again deserted, Pierre was trying to ascertain what else he could possibly do to bring Lucie back so that she would nevermore leave him and share with another man an intimacy rightfully his. He would not even have loaded his shotgun and gone after his many rivals, since it was his wife who enticed them. All he ever wanted was to see her back again once her infidelity had been consummated. Even though he was as much a heathen as a wild boar, Pierre had recently turned to the village priest for help. That very afternoon, pretending an appointment with his accountant, he had gone once again to pray secretly in the church's crypt on the tomb of the blessed Hubertine. Under the marble slab was buried a nun who had lived such a virtuous and sinless existence that more than two hundred years after her death, she could still help the hapless victims of unrequited love.

Many years ago the young nun's life had been a model of chastity and gentleness, and she had left in these parts an undying example of righteousness. Pierre would let himself dream about a wife who would be like Hubertine, a quiet and submissive spouse, a living saint, like those ethereal and beautiful women whose names could be found printed on the pages of the church calendar. Hubertine had many worshippers, and some people had even gone as far as asking her to give them back a virility that they had lost. Nobody really knew why such a pious virgin had been chosen as the patron saint of impotent men, but a few farmhands could whisper in your ear that she had indeed answered their prayers and fulfilled the desires of their most unbridled expectations.

Hence, Pierre had spent three hours fervently praying over Hubertine's grave, kneeling down on the sunken and cracked slab, resting his big calloused fists on the marble polished by two centuries of begging hands. Beseeching her to bring back Lucie, he had even taken an oath to give the parish priest a large donation if she would accede to his adjuration. Pierre was sure that such a promise was bound to sway her, since the crypt was about to be closed off for repairs. The farmer was going to be her last supplicant for a long time, and he did believe that he was more in need of Hubertine's help than was anyone else who had come to entreat her.

At two o'clock in the morning, still lying awake, Pierre was awaiting his wife with such anticipation that he had all but forgotten the distemper epidemic that was slowly killing off his horses. Hubertine must have been moved by his faith, because she finally decided that such a wretched soul was indeed deserving of her pity.

And . . . the living room door creaked faintly, as if a burglar were stealing his way into the house. The dogs had not even barked. Without any hesitation someone was cutting through the darkness and walking toward the bedroom.

Pierre immediately recognized Lucie's steps. Betraying her
presence by the muffled tread of her footsteps upon the tiled
floor, she was now hurrying toward him. Pierre slid deeper
between the sheets, pretending to be sound asleep. He tried
to keep silent and ignore her, but as he felt Lucie's body so
close to him, the farmer gave in to the irresistible sensuality
of their silent reunion. He tore his shirt open and threw the
blankets aside. They fell together upon the bed. The touch
of her burning hands inflamed him so much that he felt as if
his flesh were being branded by his own lust. Soon this ravenous and alien fever gave way to an ineffable mingling of
delight and torture. Writhing with pleasure, Pierre let his desire burst forth, as violent as the fiery course of lightning
when it thrusts itself upon the fields.

The maid had been waiting for two hours before daring
to enter Pierre's bedroom and wake him. He had overslept
again, and she thought he probably had once more drowned
his loneliness in grain alcohol the night before. But after taking a few cautious steps beyond the threshold, she rushed
back to the stairs with a piercing scream. A dozen farmhands
ran up to the second floor, and guided by her terrorized and
mute gaze, they too ventured inside the room.

The farmer was dead. His naked body lay stiff across the
bed, his eyes wide open and his ashen face set in a contorted
grin. It did not take long for the gendarmes to realize that
Pierre had not died of natural causes. His neck was marred
with the deep and bluish bruises left by his murderer's fingernails, while his chest and thighs were daubed with a thick,
brown substance, as if they had been covered by a parched
mixture of dirt and sweat. In their struggle, Pierre and his
assassin had smeared it all over the bed, for the sheets and
blankets were spattered with mud. Other traces of a more intimate nature puzzled the authorities, but were not made
public.

The next day, Lucie returned to the farm and was
greeted by the grief of the servants and the compassion of
the parish priest. She told everyone she had decided to come

home, since her cousin had recovered from his illness. Knowing perfectly well where she had actually spent the night, the gendarmes had the decency not to question her any further.

At first nobody wanted to believe it, but the news was quickly confirmed by the local newspaper and by the priest's indignant silence, caught up as he was between the bishop's decision and the animosity of his parishioners. Claiming that his church was badly deteriorated and that its foundations had become dangerously unstable, the bishop had ordered that it be temporarily closed. In the meantime, the relics preserved in its crypt would be transferred to the diocese cathedral. The farmers tried to oppose this blasphemous deportation, but it was in vain: Saint Nemorin's jawbone and Saint Agatha's heart, along with the remains of the blessed Hubertine, would be snatched away from their resting place. Trying to alleviate the villagers' resentment, the parish priest had argued that such an unexpected journey could actually help Hubertine move one step closer to sainthood, since the bishop had given him to understand that Rome was thinking of canonizing her. His parishioners were delighted at the news of such a well-deserved promotion, but they still would have preferred keeping her there among the blessed rather than losing her to the saints. A few grumbling farmers had even suggested half-jokingly that someone ought to get a pitchfork and poke a few holes in His Lordship's miter.

Well aware of the villagers' outrage, the local priest had arranged for the bishop's emissary to come to the crypt unannounced and in civilian clothes, since he was to supervise the exhumation of Hubertine's remains and their discreet transfer to the city. The parish priest had thus decided to meet him late at night, a few miles away from the village. The episcopal representative was an old and shriveled vicar, a shortsighted bookworm known for his expertise in hagiography. The priest led him into town through deserted backroads and spirited him into the church through a side entrance, which he double-locked behind them. Three workers from the city were waiting in the crypt, ready to start removing the heavy slab that guarded Hubertine's grave.

The reasons behind the transfer of the relics were made painfully obvious as the entire shrine came to life under the glare of acetylene lamps. The main pillar had caved in a few inches on its foundation and was no longer supporting the vault. The crumbly retaining walls were creviced as if they had just thawed from a thirty-year frost. The old stoneware vase containing Saint Agatha's heart was precariously leaning out of its niche, and one of the glass plates protecting Saint Nemorin's reliquary had been shattered by a piece of plaster fallen from the ceiling. The thick slab that rested upon Hubertine's tomb was cracked lengthwise, and the fact that it was almost possible to peer through the fractured stone gave every onlooker the jarring sensation of committing a despicable blasphemy. One of the cornerstones of the masonry had come undone, and the vulturous hand of an unscrupulous relic hunter could have easily reached inside and grabbed a few bones from the remains of Hubertine.

Before ordering the workers to remove the ledger, the vicar tried to ease the priest's reluctance by reassuring him of the bishop's best intentions. It had been finally decided that the village could keep Saint Nemorin's jawbone and Saint Agatha's heart. The city would keep Hubertine's body until the day of her official canonization. Then she would be returned to the village, as soon as the decrepit shrine had been remodeled and no longer presented any danger to the faithful or to the defenders of the faith alike. Grudgingly satisfied with this unearthly bargain, the priest nodded in agreement. The workers positioned themselves around the grave and started to press their crowbars under the ledger.

The priest drew the vicar to one side, and as garrulous as an Easter sermon, he proceeded to tell him the story of the blessed Hubertine. Born in 1720, she was a fifteen-year-old hunchbacked shepherdess from the hamlet of Chantebuisson. Not only was she deformed, but half of her face was sullied by a reddish birthmark. Yet she never grew weary of smiling and of spreading love for life and kindness around her, even though she had quickly become the docile target of the children's wickedness and the butt of everyone's jeers.

But what had to happen finally came to pass on a rainy autumn afternoon, as Hubertine was guiding the herd toward Mortefontaine's coomb. She heard a voice calling her name, as deep as if it had sprung out of a well. She looked around but could find no one, and there was not even a well in sight. Someone called her again, but this time it came from the sky, as if she were being tested as to the true origin of the voice. Hubertine readily understood that it was a divine revelation. She was instantly overwhelmed by the love of God. She worshipped him so that she even pictured what he looked like. His face was as austere and handsome as the old squire's whose castle towered over the hills. The very same nobleman, despite the abyss that stood between their social ranks, who would always condescend to laugh at her each time he rode through the pastures.

And the Lord continued to speak to Hubertine, telling her to come to his house. Thus, at the age of sixteen the shepherdess entered the local convent, in order to isolate herself and grind a thousand bushels of prayers on behalf of a sinful and indifferent world. She remained there until her death, a short span of nine years entirely consumed by her ardent ecstasy. Her life had set such a remarkable example that the diocese ordered that she be buried in the church of her native village.

Less than a half-century later, the angry cannon balls of the French Revolution rolled throughout the land. The convent was leveled to the ground and plowed through, as if the rebels had wanted to plant the seeds of oblivion in its furrows. The crypt and Hubertine's remains were the only things spared from the harrowing of religion, and this confirmed to all that she was indeed under the protection of God.

Solemnly emphasizing these last words, the priest concluded Hubertine's story. In the silence now made even more respectful by the reawakened presence of the young shepherdess, the workers drove the last metal wedge between the ledger and the vault. Easing their crowbars onto the stone, they slowly slid aside the two broken halves of marble, revealing the darkened mouth of the tomb. As the lamps abruptly lighted the excavation, everyone stood in amazement. There was no casket in the vault; neither was there the respectable skeleton they all expected to find. In its place, the perfectly preserved body of a naked woman lay in the grave. It looked as if someone had played a macabre and blasphemous practical joke on the bishop's representative by replacing Hubertine's remains with a fresh cadaver, irreverently lying on its stomach.

The vicar stuttered with astonishment as the parish priest dropped to his knees on the edge of the grave. But the moment of stupefaction over, they quickly dismissed the possibility of a revolting and sacreligious prank. The body was that of the young nun laid bare against the ground, with its hideous hump leaning to one side and part of its waist still girdled by the remnants of an old hair shirt. The particular chemical nature of the soil, assuredly altered by supernatural intervention, had protected her from decay. Even the color of her skin had remained unaffected by her death; she lay sprawled before their eyes as if she had just fallen asleep. The vicar could not contain his curiosity any longer. He cautiously stepped into the grave to turn her over. Yet to do so meant that he would have to touch the body, profaning its sanctity with the intimate contact of his mortal hands. But the desire to contemplate the face of this corpse now certain to be canonized proved indomitable. Sprinkling his hands with holy water, he lifted Hubertine off the ground, silently praying that she would not crumble into dust.

At once a shiver overwhelmed him, as he felt under his grip the unexpected litheness of her skin. One of her arms unfolded and stretched out, revealing the well-defined track of protruding veins. Hubertine's long fingernails had remained intact, and with a sense of growing uneasiness the vicar noticed that they were finely manicured. Everyone leaned over the excavation to help upraise the body. But when this amazing and mystifying corpse had been turned over and respectfully laid beside the grave, they all stumbled back against the wall, shrinking in horror at the sight that met their eyes.

The front of Hubertine's body was burned from her chin to her knees. The skin was still blistered and covered with scabs, as if it had just been charred by an unseen fire smoldering under her, eternalizing the agony of a monstrous and unrelenting blaze. And if the grave did not contain any visible hearth, the vicar shuddered at the thought that the cold and impassible black soil had been the silent guardian of an inexorable torture. Looking in turn at the face of the wretched shepherdess, they all felt the sickly sweet and vicious mingling of ecstasy and perversion that emanated from her smile. Averting his eyes and wishing to repel the fear that was invading him, one of the workers pointed to the inscriptions covering the underside of the slab. Unbeknownst to all, Hubertine had slept for almost two hundred years under a ledger that had once been removed, turned over, and then replaced upon her grave. The workers joined the edges of the broken stone, and after nervously adjusting his glasses, the vicar stammered as he read aloud the old epitaph.

> Here Hubertine doth Lie
> Who did Live and Die
> For Naught
> Save the Love of God.

Artfully engraved, this first inscription was followed by another, crudely gouged out of the stone.

> And whom the godless revolutionaries of 1789
> Did drag out of paradise
> To make her partake in the fyres of Hell
> And give her to taste of the Devil's lust.

Hitching a Ride

WHENEVER I open the door of Angelo's, one of the greasiest diners alongside Aubry Road, the manager grabs a bowl and two eggs, and before I even have time to open my mouth he whips them up to prepare a bacon omelet. That's what I always get. I haven't been seated for five minutes when he brings it to me, placing the dish on my table with a smile of complicity. He is so sure about me that sometimes he even chances making it beforehand. I have often wondered how many of them he must have started each time he saw me coming toward his restaurant, and how many he had to serve to docile customers because I happened to be just walking down the road that day.

For Angelo I am the "bacon omelet guy." Don't ask him if I do anything else in life other than eat omelets; he's never tried to find out. He honors me that way, and I show him my appreciation by remaining one of his faithful customers, even though I have come to dislike eggs more and more. Angelo was born in Italy, in one of the miserable shantytowns around Naples, and though he is no longer poor, his reflexes still have the quickness and vivacity bred by hunger. Keeping one eye on the greasy mess of his pans, he tags the other on the customer who might leave without paying. He takes the orders with one ear while he listens to the patrons' stories with another, as the ashes of his Gauloise cigarette hang precariously over the grill. Yet no one has ever seen them actu-

Originally published as "Le Faucheur," in Claude Seignolle, *Histoires maléfiques*, Verviers (Belgium): Gérard, 1965
© 1965 by Claude Seignolle

ally falling into the food, and it is quite a miracle if you consider that he talks out of the other side of his mouth, while constantly barking at his exasperated waitresses.

Truck drivers like to stop over at Angelo's, and they help spread the diner's reputation by meeting there from a dozen different counties. They all park their huge vehicles at their leisure, and as a boulder thrown into a brook forces the current to overflow upon its banks, their trailers clog the traffic, compelling irate motorists to chance their driving skills over the ditches and onto the surrounding potato fields. Meanwhile, inside the ebullient atmosphere of the dining room, the truckers are heartily eating and drinking, as their exuberant laughter resounds like the steely rumble of grinding gears.

Later in the afternoon the truckers usually quiet down as they share the stories of their trade. Today one of them is recounting how his truck had unexpectedly become the prey of a treacherous patch of sleet twenty miles into a mountain pass. Locked by the brakes, the wheels had become uncontrollable skates as the trailer began to swerve toward a bridge railing that was drawing nearer by the second, with nothing else in sight to prevent this mammoth of a truck from crashing through. Everyone in the room knows that road: beyond that thin railing there is only empty space and the huge void of a three-hundred-foot drop to the river below.

"I thought I'd bought the farm for good," says the driver, rolling his shoulders to better demonstrate the yawing of his runaway vehicle. A hush falls over the room as all of the truckers look quite worried, despite the reassuring presence of the narrator. At last the patch of sleet came to an end. The frozen wheels freed themselves from the iron tongs of the brakes and recovered their grip on the asphalt. After shearing off two hundred feet of railing the trailer finally came to a stop, jackknifed in the middle of the road.

There is a brief moment of horrified silence before the whole diner explodes in a thundering, relieving laughter.

"I'm telling you, I've never seen death that close!" concludes the survivor, with such conviction that Angelo ironically spits out, between the ashes and the french fries, "What you talkin' about, nobody can see death, it ain't a person!" Everyone bursts out laughing, even the man who has just narrated his frightening account.

Unnoticed by the drivers, I am the only one who is not sharing in their hilarity. I know you can really see death, and after gulping down the rest of my beer, I let my memory drift back a few years.

The highway that stretches between Vitry and Cézanne is laid on a dreary, barren plain. As if to make it lonelier, the road no longer runs through any city. Obedient to the functional imagination of its engineers, it even avoids villages. Strategic curves keep the traffic away from any distracting landscape, and left on their own the motorists find the speed of their vehicles to be their only form of entertainment, and so they drive as fast as they can. That is what I also do each time I take that road, as I surrender myself to the exhilarating hazards of a steady 100 m.p.h.

And so last July, when I found myself on this suicidal highway once again, alone in my Maserati and in need of tempering company, I did not hesitate to answer the call of a hitchhiker who was eyeing the road at the Vitry exit. Besides, even if I had not wanted to stop, he acted in such a way that I had no choice but to obey him; for if I had not jammed on the brakes, I would surely have run him over. I say I had to "obey" him because, while he stretched out his arm in a manner that haughtily designated me as his chosen means of transportation, he also deliberately stepped into the path of my car.

I let him get in and sit beside me. He was a sprightly old man with a tall, gaunt frame and a nose that resembled the blade of a pruning knife. His tousled hair was set low on his head. His skin was thick and wrinkled like bark, with dirt in every crease. He was dressed in honest farmworker clothes whose cut certainly did not follow any recognized fashion: rain-faded and sun-bleached corduroy, which looked as everlasting as time. From my observations I deduced that he was

a journeyman on his way to be hired in the fields of Brie. (But I didn't realize, although it was obvious, that nowadays Brie farmers have little use of such workers, since modern harvesting machines can perform in a single stroke the work of twenty sturdy men.) I asked him where he planned to be hired, but he did not look at me nor did he answer. He only pointed his finger to the road ahead of us, and I understood that I would get nothing more out of him. It was quite clear that he wanted me to drive on until we had reached his destination. Soon his company started to annoy me. I had agreed to give him a lift so I could have someone to talk to and thus fight the boredom of this journey, but I was now carrying a silence much worse than the feeling of isolation that prods the travelers of this road to accelerate.

Therefore, I decided to whip up the fieriness of my invisible horses, but far from being concerned, the man seemed to be more relaxed. By the time we reached 110 m.p.h., he even looked at the speedometer with a satisfaction that almost brightened his face. Disappointed, I slowed down a little and proceeded to start a monologue directed at him.

This made him instantly lose his pleasure, but I went on and told him that two days ago, in my in-laws' garden, I had accidentally broken the gardener's only scythe while mowing the lawn. So I had gone to buy a new one at an old hardware store that still sold a few of these contraptions. Eager to show me his knowledge, the owner had explained to me the different advantages of five or six kinds of scythes that he sold—advantages that I in turn described to my silent companion, who, surprised, granted me a brief but friendly glance. I then told him that during my captivity in Germany I had been forced to work in a tool factory, and I proudly informed him that in a period of two years I had turned out at least ten thousand blades of the best quality steel—the Swedish kind, whose sharpened edges could have shaved beards as well as prairies.

By now my quiet companion was looking straight at me, and I saw that he was pleased to hear me talk shop. And so I continued, describing the different cutting styles of old and illustrious mowers, those amazing nineteenth-century reapers who journeyed from oceans of corn to seas of alfalfa, driven by a cutting strength that seemed as invincible as the tide. This time the man stared at me and showed that he was listening to my soliloquy with real satisfaction. I thought that by remaining silent I might irritate him, so I proceeded to tell him how, in the fifteenth century, Saint Claude had become the patron saint of the guild, when—so claims the legend—he had inadvertently razed a whole row of poplars as if they were mere thistles. I then acknowledged to my silent but captivated passenger that I was indeed sad to see this glorious trade vanish, as if so many old-time reapers were being cut down by the dispassionate efficiency of automated blades.

At that point, the old man straightened up in his seat as if he had suddenly come to a decision. He stretched out his hand and adamantly pointed his finger at the gas gauge. I looked at it; it was on empty. I was surprised, for I had filled it up less than fifty miles before. Fortunately, we were close to an exit that advertised a gas station. I drove the car to the pump and went out to fill the tank, but after a few gallons, the gasoline surged back and overflowed. The mechanic walked up to me, and I was about to ask him to check the gas gauge when a loud clang drowned my words. I jumped back and stared at my car in disbelief: it looked as though the front end had suddenly caved into the ground, leaving the vehicle listing at a forty-five-degree angle. Both the mechanic and I kneeled down and peered underneath the car as the reason for this extraordinary accident was immediately revealed to us. The two front wheels had collapsed inwards. They were severed from their axle as if they had just been turned into dead wood.

Somewhat shaken, I struggled to my feet and walked around a little as the mechanic stared at the twisted heap of metal.

"That's the craziest thing I've ever seen," he said, wiping an oily rag across his face. "A half mile more at the speed you were driving, and you were a dead man!" I agreed with a retrospective shiver and replied that I really owed my life to my passenger, a strange but wise traveler who, just in time, had unknowingly shut one of the trapdoors of my fate.

"What traveler?" answered the mechanic, with a strange look on his face. "You were alone when you got here."

I rushed back to the car. In the commotion I had all but forgotten about the hitchhiker and I was afraid he might be hurt, but the old journeyman was no longer there. I leaned inside, searching for some trace of him, but found nothing . . . except, perhaps, a slight smell of freshly plowed earth.

Ever since that day I shudder at the thought of those drivers who have picked up and trustfully helped this death laborer, but who will never be able to testify to his existence as I have.

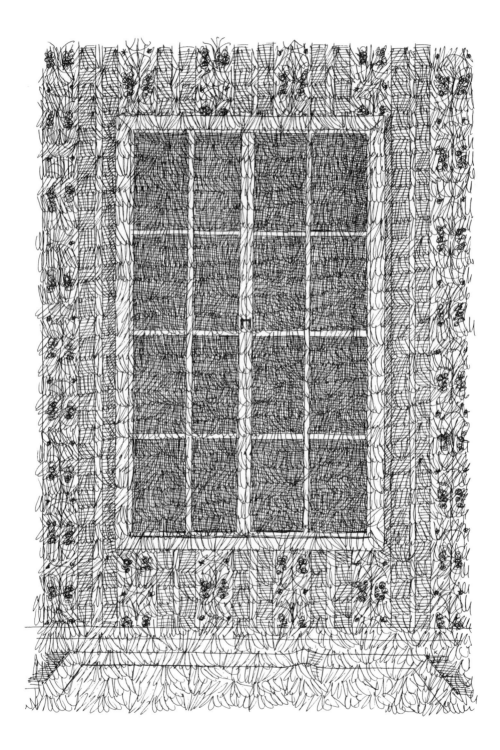

Night Horses

Traveling from Paris by train, I got off at Landivisiau in late afternoon. It was my first trip to Brittany, and the mild dampness of its weather was a welcome change from the rigors of the capital. The night was hurrying to bring the day to a close, but the streetlights still hindered the darkness from completely invading the town. And if the provincial architecture, veiled by the deepening twilight, greeted me with a startling change of surroundings, my surprise was further heightened by the folkloric attire and distinctive accent of the inhabitants.

I ate my dinner at the local hotel, and although I could have slept there on a comfortable bed, I had made up my mind to leave that very evening and press on toward my final destination. The impatience of my heart was luring me ever closer to Kerentran, where I was only expected the next day. But knowing that the night would certainly feel shorter if I slept nearer to Joceline, I had decided to reach the inn closest to her manor.

When dinner was over I inquired about any available means of transportation, but to my surprise I was curtly told that I would not find any. The man directly facing me across the table, a young and robust farmer, even chided me for my temerity. Another diner nodded in agreement, saying it was obvious that I was a stranger in these parts; otherwise, the

Originally published as "Les Chevaux de la nuit," in Claude Seignolle, *Les Chevaux de la nuit et autres récits cruels*, Verviers (Belgium): Gérard, 1967
© 1967 by Claude Seignolle

very thought of leaving the town at night would never have crossed my mind.

"Around here no one travels during the dark hours," reproached the man standing at the head of the table. "The night does not belong to the living," added another in a slightly menacing tone. As they all became quiet, their reproving silence only urged me to leave without the loss of another moment, even if it meant I would have to walk the twenty miles separating me from Kerentran.

The night was clear under the full moon. I had no difficulty finding my way, since every curve of that road had graced Joceline's last letters, making me feel as if I already knew each intersection and village . . . How many miles had I actually walked, lost in thought and dreaming of Joceline? Even to this day I could not really say. All I remember is that at some point along that road I became aware of a long, large line that seemed to be painted across the pavement. I looked up and found myself at the foot of a huge cross towering over a wayside shrine. It was its shadow, reflected upon the road, which had caught my attention and drawn me out of my reverie. Then, in the distance, cutting through the softness of the night, I heard the oncoming rattle of a carriage. I stopped and sighed with relief, blessing the apparition of this unexpected traveler, since I felt certain that for a few francs he would take me all the way to Kerentran.

I could now see its contours. Drawn by three white horses harnessed in an arrowhead formation, it was approaching very rapidly. Oddly enough the horses' hooves were not shod, and their gallop resounded upon the rocky surface of the pavement like the muffled beat of a huge wooden heart. Stepping onto the road, I waved and shouted at the driver, but despite the vigor of my calls he failed to notice me. The coach was now bearing down on me without slowing in its course. I jumped aside and barely had time to dodge the lash of a whip, which cracked above my head like a snarling animal.

I was outraged and could not refrain from shouting an

insult, but then, within a few yards, the fiery horses came to a screeching halt. At the speed they were going, even the most intrepid driver could not have stopped them in a hundred yards without snapping the reins. I was startled, and I hesitated to walk up to the coach for fear I'd be thrashed by the driver. Finally, after uttering a few words of apology, I took a few steps forward. The coachman was standing up against the slatted side of the carriage, staring straight in front of him. A stocky man dressed in a brown cape, he was as petrified as a rock. I could not see his features hidden under a large brimmed hat, but I discovered that he had two traveling companions, clothed in the same fashion, who sat astride the two horses hitched up behind the yoke, while the lead horse remained free of riders. It looked as if the driver had absolutely no notion as to the proper way of harnessing a carriage. I did try to ask them a few questions, but despite the insistence of my pleas, none of them even turned their heads to look at me. Indeed, the whole equipage, men and horses alike, remained as motionless as statues.

However, they were on the only road to Kerentran, and since they did not seem to have any objections, I no longer hesitated and climbed into the back of their carriage. Almost instantly I was overcome by a noisome stench of burnt meerschaum and the fetid smell of rotten leather. Right at my feet, lying down on the loose planks of the floor and seemingly indifferent to the surrounding stink, a human form was sound asleep. I did not have the leisure to examine it any closer; with a thrashing lash of his whip, the driver abruptly set his horses in motion, and I had to grab onto the sideboards to avoid being thrown out onto the road.

We drove on at such a speed that despite my efforts, I was shoved several times against my sleeping companion. As he did not awake, I suddenly became frightened that the driver and his strange acolytes might well have perpetrated a crime. But I did not have time to entertain this thought much longer, for what happened next proved to be even more mystifying. We had covered about three miles when our vehicle unexpectedly left the main road. The dexterity of the driver was beyond belief, for in the hands of anyone else the carriage could not have accomplished such a right-angle maneuver without overturning.

A few hundred yards ahead I saw the lighted windows of a huge farmhouse. We stopped so suddenly that I nearly cracked my skull against one of the iron posts. The driver's attendants quickly dismounted and ran toward the house. They flung the door open and entered a large room. Inside, a few people were gathered around a wide brass bed upon which slept an old woman. But to my surprise, no one in the room seemed even to acknowledge the presence of the two intruders. They both walked up to the bed and grabbed the woman by her feet and her shoulders. She woke up with a start and tried to resist, but after uttering a few raucous shouts she quickly stopped struggling. Silent and lifeless, she was then removed from the house, whisked away to the carriage, and unceremoniously heaved over the sideboards. She fell beside me with a nauseating thud and remained as motionless as the other sleeping traveler.

As if they had been suddenly awakened, the people standing in the farmhouse drew nearer to the bed and started to moan and cry, while the dogs, who had not even noticed our tumultuous arrival, began to howl from inside their kennels. In utter dismay I then distinctly saw the old woman, still lying on her bed, unconcerned by the tears of her grieving family, as pale as if she were dead, while she was in fact also lying at my feet.

I was aghast. I tried in vain to jump out and run away, but the two attendants had already remounted their horses, and in an instant the coach was rattling its way back onto the dirt road. I pleaded with the driver and begged him to let me go, but he continued to ignore my presence. We drove on through the night for hours before he finally stopped his horses on the outskirts of a small village. Still gazing at the road, the driver consented to talk to me for the first time.

"You asked me to drive to Kerentran, therefore I will, but be patient. I can only go there two days from now, and by then the young lady of the manor should be ready for us . . ."

he said with a growl, as if his words were the muffled menace
of a cornered animal. And as he raised his arm to whip the
horses, the brim of his hat lifted for a brief moment. I caught
sight of his face, of his wasted and gaunt features, his mouth
wide open, and the whites of his eyes, in which no pupils
could be found.

I jumped out of the carriage and escaped, running
madly through the fields in search of the nearest house.

The eerie equipage was already far away when I reached
the first house of the village. There I stood, banging in vain
against a door that was as muted and hostile as the night. Yet
I knew that behind that door someone had heard me, for a
cry of surprise, quickly muffled, had answered my first knock.

In a panic I rushed to the next house, where I resumed
my frantic rapping on its door. (Today I must confess it was
only the hope of finding the protection of four solid walls
that kept my blood running in my veins.)

"Open up, for God's sake, open up," I finally screamed
in despair, having recovered the use of my voice. To hear me
so distraught suddenly changed the minds of those barri-
caded inside. Someone cracked the door at last, and the faltering light of a candle revealed a man's face, contorted with
fear.

"Who . . . Who are you?" he stammered, while trying to
identify me. I answered that I was a guest of the earl of Kerentran and that I had become lost on my way to the manor.

The door finally opened wide enough, and I was ushered
inside. A few minutes later, standing by a huge hearth, I
was still trying to collect myself as my host reawakened the
choking, yet comforting, smoke of a dormant fire. His wife
brought me a kitchen glass full of brandy. I drank it in long
draughts, but I was so shaken that I barely felt its bite. I had
to disburden myself of this nightmare, and I proceeded to
tell them my story. But as I was speaking and gradually pulling myself together, I noticed that my hosts were growing
even more apprehensive.

"I knew I had recognized the rattle of that carriage,"

sighed the man. "When you started knocking at our door I thought it was *He* who was coming for one of us." Lowering his voice to a whisper, he told me I had traveled in the company of the *Ankou*, the dreaded death laborer and his two servants from the nether world.

I was so astonished that I even mustered a smile, thinking he had chosen to allay my fears by making me the butt of a practical joke. But to my dismay I soon realized that my host was not the least inclined to be humorous. Retracing the events of my journey, he informed me that we had stopped in the village of Kernoter to "take charge" of Mrs. Loarrer, an old charwoman sapped by an incurable disease. And since the carriage had also passed through the town of Plougouvest after my escape, it could only mean that Death had snatched away the soul of Christophe Ropartz, a local lumberjack who had been agonizing all day after being felled by a young and vengeful oak tree.

Still unconvinced although I could not find a more reassuring explanation for the events that I had witnessed, I chided my host for what I took to be a local and ridiculous superstition.

"Surely you don't expect me to believe this," I answered him. "At worst we are dealing here with a team of unscrupulous thieves, the kind that would desecrate an isolated tomb for the mere gain of a few gold teeth." And in the hope of comforting them I proceeded with a meticulous description of the carriage and its bizarre, but definitely earthly, proprietors. As if to exorcise my own childish fears I described the driver in as many details as I could. Despite his rude behavior and his frightening looks, I assured them that he was quite alive—indeed, too much for my comfort. I even told them of his intentions to drive to Kerentran in a couple of days. My host immediately crossed himself and shrank deeper into his seat.

"By the Blessed Virgin, you *did* see him!" he shuddered. "The man you have just described is Hervé Lenn, from the hamlet of Plouzedené, who died in December; and since he was the last one of the year to pass away, he is now by right the *Ankou* of the entire county for one year. You have provoked him," my host continued. "He allowed you to escape with your life, but now he is forced to claim someone else's, according to the precepts of his charge . . . The young lady from Kerentran is foredoomed; there is nothing anyone can do about it."

Stunned by the distress of this man and by the grief of his wife, who punctuated his story with mournful nods of assent, I was suddenly overwhelmed by the frightful truth of this tale, as I slumped in an armchair and abandoned myself to the grim reality of their rustic fears. We spent the rest of the night around the crackling glitter of the hearth, frantically poking its embers. We looked at one another surreptitiously, each time rekindling our fears, each time deepening our restlessness. It was no use trying to sleep, for we all had a desperate need to feel that we were indeed alive, still alive among the living. The slightest noise from outside would suddenly make us stare at the door with such intensity that the mere settling of the burning logs was enough to startle us.

Dawn came at last. I was freed by the first rays of the sun, as if a thick, dark yoke had been lifted from my shoulders. I took leave of my hosts without a word, abandoning them in a shelter still enmeshed by the lingering shroud of night. I walked back through the fields and soon reached the road, trying to collect myself as I strode toward Kerentran. But in spite of the invigorating smell of freshly cut grass and the soothing ebullience of a nearby brook, the words of Hervé Lenn, the *Ankou*, continued to torment me, darkening my soul as I walked under the morning sun.

I was exhausted when I arrived at the manor. Upon discovering that I had made the journey on foot, Joceline's parents wondered if I had all my senses. As previously arranged, they had sent a coach to Landivisiau Station, and the driver had waited in vain for me to get off the morning train. I managed to explain my actions by pretending there had been some sort of misunderstanding, and I only told them a

half-truth when I said that in fact I had arrived the night before, and thinking that I still was quite a good walker, I had
decided to do without the coach.

At last Joceline appeared on the threshold, and I became
oblivious of anyone else. Departing from her usual self-
restraint, she almost ran across the living room, and I took
her in my arms as if I were already protecting her. The
warmth of her yearning and the tenderness of her attentions
finally broke the spell of helplessness that had taken hold of
me the night before. Indeed, the reality of her presence reawakened my natural inclination to hold my ground and de-
fend myself. After lunch, I felt so completely restored in my
strength that I started planning a strategy. Since I knew of
the plans of the *Ankou*, I could easily deceive him. In fact, I
had two whole days ahead of me to take Joceline away from
this entire accursed province and guard her against this hell-
born reaper and his archaic ways of harvesting the lives of
frightened peasants. This primitive ritual was well-confined
within the borders of Brittany, and besides, Hervé Lenn was
only the *Ankou* of a small county, lost amidst the reality of
modern-day France.

I had long decided to keep this incredible adventure to
myself and not to alarm anyone with a secret only I could
comprehend. Thus I waited until after dinner, and pretending a pressing need to return to Paris for an important busi-
ness transaction, I told Joceline's family we would be leaving
in a few hours. The earl of Kerentran, accustomed to the
strict manners of the old French nobility, scowled at my au-
dacity. I quickly added that by a happy coincidence this journey would also allow Joceline to visit with my mother for a
few days, before she left for her summer residence on the
Riviera. I sensed that the earl was not entirely convinced,
since he still appeared to be quite displeased. Yet his wife
came unexpectedly to my aid, for she could readily attune
herself to the heart and wishes of my mother. With a few
soothing words and an indulgent look, she finally won her
husband's reluctant approval.

That night, even though I felt reassured after we had

boarded the train, listening to the power of mechanical horses that could have easily outdistanced the *Ankou*'s carriage, I sensed only too well that from this moment on, Joceline's destiny would be measured according to my strength.

Two days later we were in Paris, and even though I could have eased my vigilance, my mind was still weighing each of the alternatives that I had retained in order to better thwart the *Ankou*'s plans. Finally I decided to contact an old friend who owned a discreet penthouse in the heart of the capital. Soon I had in my hands the keys to what would become our shelter. Situated on the top floor of an old building on Saint Louis Island, the place looked impregnable. It also had the distinct advantage of resembling many similar penthouses that crowded the crests of the surrounding buildings. Seen from afar, the apartment was lost amidst an intricate maze of roof tiles and chimneys. Even a bird flying overhead could not have recognized it. Niched at the top of the building, its entrance had been painted the same color as the staircase, and when I reached the very last floor, I even had some difficulty finding my way to the penthouse, since its access door blended perfectly into the wall, as if it were a secret passageway.

That night we dined early in an out-of-the-way restaurant, and at the end of our meal I told Joceline that we would spend the evening in the company of old friends who resided on Saint Louis Island. I hailed a hackney, and in my haste I pushed Joceline into the cab. She sat down silently with a look of stupefaction upon her face, but as we drove on past the riverbank she was no longer able to contain her indignation. For the past two days Joceline had stoically endured my decidedly odd behavior, but this last turn of events was more than she could tolerate. She stared at me and insisted that I explain my actions. I evaded her questions and curtly mumbled a vague and irritated reply, which brought sparkles of tears to her eyes. How I wished I could have taken her in my arms and comforted her dismay. But to tell the truth would only have meant to torment her even more. I did not want to betray my own increasing anguish, and I had to force myself to remain silent.

It was already dark when we reached our destination. Looking onto a narrow street, the building was a high stone-made structure, lost among the accumulated mass of marble and granite that protects the heart of Paris as if it were a vault. As I looked back upon the complicated and exhaustive schemes I had elaborated for the past two days, including my most pessimistic expectation of the night yet to come, I had to admit that even the splitting asunder of the six bridges that linked the island to the rest of the world would have been a superfluous precaution. Hervé Lenn, the backward *Ankou* of Plouzenedé, would have become utterly lost outside of his uncivilized county. He could not even have driven any closer than two hundred miles from the gates of Paris.

When we reached the last floor, I had to use all of my matches in order to find the keyhole in the recessed entrance. Expecting to see my friends welcome us, Joceline became frightened and started to step back. I had to pull her inside as I slammed the door behind us. The heavy wooden panel felt as massive as a graveyard slab. I wanted to retain the protection afforded us by the darkness, and thus I resisted turning on the lights. Joceline was appalled. She freed herself from my grip, took a few steps, stumbled against a piece of furniture, and fell to the floor with a muffled cry. She trembled as I took her in my arms to try and calm her fears. I swore to her that against all appearances I had not taken leave of my senses. I did all I could to convince her: I said there was a last secret left within me, something I could not explain at the moment, but I beseeched her to trust me, to remain there until midnight, and for the duration of that time not to ask me any of the questions to which she was more than entitled. I begged her to stay, insisting that there was indeed reason enough for my aberrant behavior, and I assured her that soon after midnight I would readily explain the motives behind my conduct. With reluctance she finally acceded to my request, and after much groping about I found a large sofa where we both lay down. Joceline cuddled against me, gently sobbing on my shoulder, while an impenetrable darkness draped our shelter like a veil.

Minute by minute the hours were slipping by, each one greeted by the pounding of my heart, each once sanctioned by the soft and crystalline chime of an invisible clock. There only remained half an hour until midnight when suddenly, cutting through the night, the sound of loud stamping echoed from the street. I stood up in a frenzy and violently shook Joceline from her sleep, pressing my hand over her mouth to keep her from screaming. My heart was thudding with fear, as if it were following the rhythm of the hooves that at once I had recognized. The stampede stopped as abruptly as it had begun, and it rendered the ensuing silence even more petrifying. The *Ankou* had come! Against all odds he had found us. Nothing could possibly deter him: neither the distance nor the place nor the time could keep him from his appointed rounds!

But despite my horror, I was not one to be vanquished so easily. It was obvious that no manmade weapon would have any effect on the ghost of Hervé Lenn or on his two attendants from beyond the grave. However, I sensed that perhaps I could propitiate them, offering myself in the place of Joceline, thereby ensuring the *Ankou* that he would leave Paris with the exact number of souls he had come to gather. I then frantically searched in the dark for a hiding place, and at last I found the panels of a high cupboard. I opened it at once and tried to force Joceline to hide there, but she desperately fought back to remain by my side. I had no time left to argue—I pushed her inside with a violent heave and locked the cupboard behind her.

I hurried back to the door, stumbling in the dark against unseen pieces of furniture, finding my way by groping alongside the wall. There I waited, shaking like a leaf but resolute in my heart, bracing myself against the moment to come. I was not so much distraught by the imminence of my death as I was by the thought of leaving Joceline behind, confronting alone this incomprehensible nightmare. And yet, after a few agonizing minutes, the impossible took place. Like a sudden squall sweeping across the street, I heard the night horses resume their baleful stampede. They were leaving . . . they were gone! The *Ankou* had run out of time before he could find the door! I stumbled back into the room, catching my breath and crying like a child. I located the cupboard, unlocked the panels, and reached for Joceline.

My hands found nothing. Yet my eyes and ears unraveled at once this mystery. Screaming with despair, I realized I was facing the night itself, the deep and frozen void concealed behind this window through which I had hurled Joceline to her death.

Selected Bibliography

WORKS BY CLAUDE SEIGNOLLE

Short stories and novels

Le Bahut noir. Paris: Le Terrain Vague, 1958.

La Brume ne se lèvera plus. Paris: Le Terrain Vague, 1959.

Les Chevaux de la nuit et autres récits cruels. Verviers (Belgium): Gérard, 1967.

Le Chupador. Paris: Editions Pédagogiques Modernes, 1960. (With twenty-two illustrations by Sergio Moyano.)

Contes macabres. Verviers (Belgium): Gérard, 1966.

Contes sorciers. Verviers (Belgium): Gérard, 1974.

Un Corbeau de toutes couleurs. Paris: Denoël, 1962.

Delphine. Paris: Editions Morgan, 1971.

Le Diable en sabots. Paris: Le Terrain Vague, 1959.

Le Diable en sabots et Le Rond des sorciers. Geneva: Slatkine reprints, 1981.

L'Evènement. Paris: Le Terrain Vague, 1960.

Le Gâloup. Paris: Editions Pédagogiques Modernes, 1960. (With twenty-two reproductions from the Cabinet des Estampes Collection of the Bibliothèque Nationale.)

Histoires maléfiques. Verviers (Belgium): Gérard, 1965.

Histoires vénéneuses. Paris: Pierre Belfond, 1970.

L'Homme qui ne pouvait mourir. In Collection du XXe siècle. Anvers (Belgium): Walter Beckers, 1969.

Invitation au château de l'étrange. Paris: Maisonneuve & Larose, 1969.

"Invitation au château de l'étrange." In Alain Vircondelet, *La Poésie fantastique française*. Paris: Seghers, 1973. (Anthology.)

Les Loups verts et autres cruautés guerrières. Verviers (Belgium): Gérard, 1970.

Les Malédictions. In Les Maîtres du fantastique traditionnel.
   Paris: Maisonneuve & Larose, 1963.
La Malvenue. Paris: Maisonneuve, 1952.
Marie la louve. Paris: Domat-Monchrestien, 1949.
La Nuit des Halles. Paris: Maisonneuve & Larose, 1965. (With a
   lithograph by Victor Lefebvre.)
Oeuvres de Claude Seignolle. In Richesses du folklore de France,
   23 volumes. Paris: Les Presses de la Renaissance, 1976–79.
Le Rond des sorciers. Paris: Editions des Quatre-Vents, 1945.

Ethnology and Folklore

Le Berry traditionnel. In Collection documentaire de folklore.
   Paris: Maisonneuve & Larose, 1969.
Contes populaires de Guyenne. In Les Littératures populaires de
   toutes les nations. Paris: Maisonneuve & Larose, 1971.
Le Diable dans la tradition populaire. In Collection documentaire
   de folklore de tous les pays. Paris: Besson & Chantemerle,
   1959.
Les Evangiles du Diable. Paris: Pierre Belfond, 1967. (Condensed edition.)
Les Evangiles du Diable selon la croyance populaire. In Les Littératures populaires de toutes les nations. Paris: Maisonneuve
   & Larose, 1964. (Original edition, 928 pages. Subsequent
   editions are condensed.)
Le Folklore de la Provence. In Contributions au folklore des
   provinces de France. Paris: Maisonneuve & Larose, 1963.
Le Folklore de la Provence. In Contributions au folklore des
   provinces de France. Nouvelle édition. Paris: Maison-
   neuve & Larose, 1967.
Le Folklore du Hurepoix. In Contributions au folklore des prov-
   inces de France. Paris: Maisonneuve, 1937.
Le Folklore du Hurepoix. Nouvelle édition. Paris: Maisonneuve &
   Larose, 1978.
Le Folklore du Languedoc. In Contributions au folklore des prov-
   inces de France. Paris: Besson & Chantemerle, 1960.
Le Folklore du Languedoc. Nouvelle édition. Paris: Maisonneuve
   & Larose, 1977.
Les Fouilles de Robinson. In Contributions à l'étude des origines
   parisiennes. Paris: Maisonneuve, 1945.
Histoires et légendes de la Gascogne et de la Guyenne mystérieuses.

Textes recueillis et présentés par Claude Seignolle. In Histoires et légendes. Paris: Tchou, 1973.
Histoires et légendes du Diable. In Histoires et légendes. Paris: Tchou, 1973.
Pierres à légende de la montagne bourbonnaise. Evreux: Devé, 1934.
En Sologne. In Collection documentaire de folklore de tous les pays. Paris: Maisonneuve, 1945.
En Sologne: Moeurs et coutumes. Nouvelle édition. Paris: Maisonneuve & Larose, 1967.

Autobiography

La Gueule. Anvers (Belgium): Walter Beckers, 1964.
Un Homme nu. Paris: Editions Pédagogiques Modernes, 1961.
Lithos et moi: Souvenirs d'une enfance archéologique. Paris: Le Terrain Vague, 1960.

WORKS ON CLAUDE SEIGNOLLE

Doyon, René-Louis. *A la Recherche du vrai à travers l'oeuvre de Claude Seignolle*. Paris: La Connaissance, 1959.
Durand-Tullou, A. *Du Chien au loup-garou dans le fantastique de Claude Seignolle*. In Collection documentaire de folklore de tous les pays. Paris: Besson & Chantemerle, 1961.
Gilles, Raymond. *Le Folklore de la peur chez Claude Seignolle*. Mémoire de licence de philologie romane, Université libre de Bruxelles, 1974.
Jacquemin, Georges. *Claude Seignolle*. Vieux-Virton (Belgium): Editions de la Dryade, 1966.
Juin, Hubert. "Du Fantastique en littérature: L'Exemple de Claude Seignolle." In *Chroniques sentimentales*. Paris: Mercure de France, 1962.
Planque, Bernard. *Un Aventurier de l'insolite: Claude Seignolle*. Périgueux: Fanlac, 1960.
Rousseaux, André. *Terroirs et diableries de Claude Seignolle*. Paris: Editions Pédagogiques Modernes, 1960.